Stalker

Short Stories and True Adventures

Heather Rath

Manor House

Library and Archives Canada
Cataloguing in Publication

Title: Stalker - short stories and true adventures / Heather Rath.

Names: Rath, Heather, author.

Identifiers: Canadiana 20230572952 |

ISBN 9781998938056 (hardcover) |

ISBN 9781998938049 (softcover)

Subjects: LCGFT: Short stories. | LCGFT: Anecdotes.

Classification: LCC PS8585.A832 S73 2023 | DDC
C818/.54—dc23

Note: This collection of Fiction and Non-fiction works has
protected the privacy of individuals. Any resemblance to
locations or persons alive or dead is purely coincidental.

Front Cover art: Motortion / Shutterstock / (Eye at Keyhole)
Back Cover art: Heather Rath (photo of Author)

First Edition
Cover Design-layout / Interior- layout: Michael Davie
200 pages / 56,000 words.   All rights reserved.

Published 2023 / Copyright 2023
Manor House Publishing Inc.
452 Cottingham Crescent, Ancaster, ON, L9G 3V6
www.manor-house-publishing.com (905) 648-4797

Funded by the Government of Canada | Canadä

3

With love to my remarkable family especially my husband and best friend, Norm, who doubles as my back-office support.

And loving gratitude to Gloria and Ted Ingram.

Acknowledgements:

So many have added to my growth:

First, my thanks to you the reader - this book wouldn't be possible without you. It's fun writing the stories but it's even more fun to share them with an appreciative audience.

Sincere thanks to Mike Davie of Manor House who believed in my talent and took the time to guide me through the process.

A grateful thank you to:

My writing tribe near and far, especially the Bluewater Writers: Bob Boulton, Delia Petrucci-DeSantis, Mary Frost, Phyllis Humby, Bob McCarthy, Karen McIlwaine, Rhonda Melanson, Kathy Milliken, Lynn Tait, Najah Shuqair.

My original WIT (Writers in Transition) mentors: Debbie Okun Hill, Josephine Ryan, Peggy Fletcher, John Drage, Hope Morritt, Carmen Ziolkowski, Anne Beachey, Norma West Linder.

My former colleagues/writers/friends: Marlyn Horsdal, Peter Snow, Ritchie With

To all those I have met on our travels throughout the world who have contributed to my growth and belief in the goodness of mankind.

- Heather Rath

Foreword / The Author's Confession

"You must have a dark side," claimed a judge after reading one of my award-winning short stories.

I thought about that: Do I?

Yes, I do. But then I always believed most people have two sides. One they present to the public. One they keep hidden away lest others be critical and think less of them. This side is shared only with your closest friends and family.

Suddenly I became fascinated with --- and began to research --- the dual sides idea: dark vs light, negative vs positive. I've come to the conclusion we all have two sides, whether we acknowledge them or not.

So my award-winning short stories happen to be on the dark side. And perhaps that is why they have been recognized. It's difficult sometimes to write about the dark side. But it's equally as difficult to write about the light side that could easily become the dark side.

Most of my 'dark' stories are a slice of the unknown. Aren't we all afraid of the dark? Writing about the down side of life brings those fears to light. And my imagination, *your* imagination, knows no bounds. If you, like me, tend to catastrophize events that most likely will not happen, well, welcome to the dark side.

In my case, the lighter side of life is equally as important as the darker side. For instance, the travel vignettes you find in this book often linger on the lighter side. It took me years to get to that stage.

Once upon a time the idea of leaving Canada and travelling abroad terrified me. I suffered from extreme culture shock. Couldn't eat. Couldn't sleep. Panic attacks. Not the usual way you want to spend time in a foreign country.

On the other hand, my husband hit the ground running in a foreign country. Loved the challenge of unfamiliarity: not knowing the language, finding accommodation without a prior booking.

Needless to say, I was the reluctant traveller. So why would I go to these off-the-beaten-track locations, like the Amazon Jungle or Amman in Jordan or Lhasa in Tibet, that he embraced with fervent joy? Why subject myself to this highest form of fear? Why expose myself to the dark side?

Because deep down inside me I knew I wanted to experience my own unadulterated delight in exploring a culture other than my own. But I needed to reach that comfort zone by myself. It took years, leaning on him for support, before I reached that level of his joy.

One year, when I suggested we go to Viet Nam, he looked at me with agreeable surprise. I knew then I had finally conquered my fear.

Without travelling, I would never experience my first mouth-watering seafood *ceviche* in an Old World restaurant setting in Lima, Peru, or dine on blue-skin chicken, its blood used for a nourishing side of soup, in Beijing, or consume *tartar de carne* (minced raw beef with seasonings) in a Paris bistro after which I suffered a debilitating bout of stomach sickness.

Independent travelling introduced me to the kindness of people worldwide and enriched my appreciation of new adventures. It also introduced me to those who take advantage of a foreigner in new territory... like the carpet peddler in Istanbul who pestered and followed us, insisting we share the name of our hotel in case we changed our mind to buy.

I invite you to join me as together we navigate the dark side and the light side in this original collection of both.

-   **Heather Rath**

Table of Contents:

Praise for *Stalker*...

"Heather Rath's stories are clearly well crafted. The language is untainted, and she builds and shapes the characters with well suited traits. She is discreet with hints of surprise throughout the body of the story, cleverly dropping the most appropriate ending in the last few lines, leaving the reader to ponder in total amazement."

- **Delia De Santis**, author, *Fast Forward and Other Stories*

"From experience, I believe that some journalists think they know it all but fail miserably when trying to "craft" a story into captivating, very readable fiction, and sometimes even informative articles. Not Heather Rath. With her vivid imagination, creativity, knowledge of her diverse subjects, and ability to paint word pictures -- whether of a green iguana or ladies skinny-dipping -- Heather's artistic roots are well used in her work. As a world traveler, rather than just a tourist, she gives us first-hand glimpses of life in various pockets of the globe. Shake on a little humour and sense of fun, and you have a volume of many enjoyable reads here."

-- **Ritchie With**; journalist, editor, blogger and business writer.

"Heather Rath is a skilled writer whose work is always engaging. Her short fiction pieces are tightly constructed and well-paced, and often deliver an unexpected shock. She and her husband are enthusiastic travellers, mostly off the beaten track in exotic locales, and Heather describes their adventures -- and yes, misadventures -- with insight and humour. Luckily for readers they have, so far, survived their quests. This collection of Heather's intriguing fiction, lively memoir and enjoyable travel accounts is entertaining and informative. Don't miss it!"

- **Marlyn Horsdal**, author, *Sweetness from Ashes* and *The Judge and the Lady*

"Heather Rath's short stories walk us through travels real and fictitious, leading us through pages of mundane rituals of everyday life. Then they veer off into the surreal and the macabre using sex and suspense that tickles our curiosity leaving us biting our nails, then leading us to the edge of proverbial cliffs. We want to look away but at the same time we crave more."

- **Lynn Tait** author of *You Break It You Buy It*

"Heather Rath has renewed my appreciation for short stories. Each tale in this entertaining and often titillating collection has its own unique voice with unforgettable characters. From dry-humoured wit to suspense, each story's dilemmas, solved or not, are delivered in an unpredictable manner that delights me."

- **Phyllis L Humby**, author, novels *On The Rock – and Old Broad Road* and memoir *Hazards of the Trade: An intimate reveal of the 80s and 90s lingerie boom*

"Heather Rath has penned a tapestry of personal escapades spiced with a few gritty works of fiction all with a keen eye on life's fellow travellers. At times posing as pages torn from a travel diary, the author leads us through self-deprecating, humorous and often touching observations on her *camino de la vida*. From contemplating mortality in a Mayan sweat lodge to watching her partner's abduction by a love-struck orangutan in Borneo. The memories flow like cocktail conversations with old friends. Crafted with sharp, dark turns to entertain, Heather's prize winning fiction will tease and titillate your imagination."

Peter Snow, Ph.D. journalist, filmmaker and media consultant

About Stalker:

Stalker invites the reader to take a journey into two worlds: the dark and light sides of life.

Frightening, suspenseful moments in award-winning short stories co-exist with true-life adventure vignettes: a blend of truth and fiction.

The stories explore the mind's hidden fears and desires while the vignettes deliver a slice of reality, sometimes with unexpected conclusions. They are snapshots of experiences in different cultures through the eyes -- and writings – of an insightful world traveller.

About the Author:

Since winning a city-wide writing contest for elementary students in Ottawa, Canada, Heather Rath knew writing would be a major part of her life.

When she grew up, she was sequentially a reporter, editor of a weekly newspaper and a monthly business magazine before becoming head of communications for a multi-national company. During this time, she edited, and contributed to, two anthologies of southwestern Ontario writers.

An award-winning writer, she has been published widely over the years in various publications and some of her work for children has been translated into Braille.

She is a member of CANSCAIP (Canadian Society of Children's Authors, Illustrators & Performers), Canadian Authors Association and an associate member of Crime Writers of Canada.

Family, writing, and travel are her passions. Sometimes she's not good at juggling all three. She invites you to visit her website at www.heatherrath.net.

PART ONE:

Unsettling Short Stories

14

Drako

I love reptiles.

My parents hate them.

They warned me---repeatedly---*no snakes, frogs, or other reptiles in this house…ever!*

Otherwise, I'm sure my parents would kill me.

I'm allergic to fur. As a developing artist at 15, I need to study---and draw--- real, live animals and people. Only it's hard to find people to pose. They don't like sitting or standing still for a long time.

Was hanging around a pet shop in our neighborhood. I spy this sign speaking directly to me: "Allergic to fur? We have the right pet for you!"

Donning my facemask against germs, I enter. Masked salesman quickly approaches. Toady-looking guy with a croaky throat. Waves me over to a small section of the shop by the fish. Points out a large aquarium. Home to various scaly, creepy-looking creatures doing nothing much but hanging out on a hot rock. Salamanders, bug-eyed red toads, fancy-bearded dragon, leopard gecko, veiled chameleon, Bahaman anole, Pacman frog, long-tailed lizard.

And then, this beauty. In an aquarium all by himself. Caught my eye with just the slightest move. A green iguana from some tropical forest. Depending on where you looked, his green skin changed different shades. Awesome. You'd never find any magnificent creature like this in Ontario.

Fell in love immediately. Called him Drako. Stunning. With his long tail, he easily measured three feet. Flicked his tongue while I looked him over carefully.

"What's he eat?" I ask the toady guy.

"He's a vegetarian, kid. Likes to nibble on lettuce, grapes, even houseplant leaves…easy to feed him. Jist gotta watch he won't escape. Fast like lightning." He pauses. "Thinkin' of getting' him?"

"Ah, man, love to. Gotta check my finances first. Only have a part-time job at Food Basics. Need an aquarium, too?"

"Yep. And them's expensive, kid. Gotta get one large enough for the critter. And a hot rock, too. These fellas need heat. Specially here up north."

I nod. "Expect to sell him fast?"

"Ya never know these days. What with this virus and all, people are doin' strange things. We can't keep puppies in stock. Gone as soon's we get 'em. But this here iguana? Somehow don't think too many folks are lookin' for this green guy. Can't cuddle him. But he's neat to watch."

"And he's beautiful," I add. "Look at the different colours of green on his skin."

"Uh huh," says Toady-man. Not convinced, I can tell.

"How much?"

"One hundred dollars. Plus his aquarium."

"Look, man, I've been lookin' all over for a pet like this. I can afford him. Take good care of him, too."

"Ya want I should mark him sold?"

"Uh huh," I nod.

Jog home. My two bros are on screens. Dad not home yet. Mom in kitchen. Work on her first.

"Just found this neatest pet. A mini-dragon."

No reaction. She's watching the small counter top TV. Looking at ingredients for a Mexican recipe. Eating South of the Border for some reason lately.

"Hmmmm?" she says, pulling her head in my direction. Cigarette hangs out of her red lipstick mouth.

"Found a non-consequential pet for me. No trouble for you. He's even vegetarian."

"Sounds good to me, Rory-kins. He big?" She turns back to the mini-TV.

"No. He fits in an aquarium and I'll clean it."

"Can't be too big, then."

"He's not."

"Uh huh." Still concentrating on the TV recipe.

I go through a similar conversation with my dad. When he comes home, he's tired wearing a mask all day, mixes a cocktail of some kind, sinks in a stupor into his favorite living room chair.

"What your mom say?" he squints through his glasses at his smartphone after he half listens to me.

"As long as I clean the aquarium, she says no problem."

"Okay, then. What is it? A fish?"

Just then his smartphone rings. I disappear.

Jog back to the pet shop. Tell Toadman. "Help me choose the right aquarium for him."

That night I hop with excitement in my bedroom. Find a suitable place atop my desk and sit there thinking…wow! Tomorrow! Finally! A pet! Of my own choosing! Sooo excited.

Next day everyone's busy doing whatever it is they do each day. No-one's paying attention to me. Bike this time to the pet shop with my backpack and a carrier. Bike home again with the goods.

Haul the extra-large aquarium with the hot rock and the Drako container to my bedroom. Set up the tank. Plug in the hot rock. Close my bedroom door.

Carefully carry the Drako box to the tank. Coax him gently into the aquarium. Watch him flick his tongue. Explore.

Am ecstatic. He fascinates.

Sometime later, I decide to slowly remove the aquarium top. Touch his cool skin and marvel.

Like lightning, Drako leaps from the hot rock to the log in the aquarium to the top of the tank. He's out!

I know he's arboreal so I look up.

Scan top of the curtained windows. He's there! Thinks he's hiding but his long tail hangs down. Already I love his personality.

He scurries along the wooden curtain rod.

Sudden steps on the stairs. Panic!

Mom enters my room.

"Rory…what the hell…?" she raises her voice. Sees the aquarium. Looks up. Sees Drako. Screams.

Mom still screaming. Dad rushes in.

"What the…?"

Looks up. Spies Drako. Mouth opens wide. Grabs my baseball bat in the corner. Raises his arm and takes aim.

"No!" I yell.

He swings the bat with great force. Misses Drako. Hits me bulls-eye on the head.

More screaming.

Told you my parents would kill me.

---Winner, 2020, Ligonier Valley Writers Flash Fiction Contest

Kill Bill

I lie in a semi-comatose state, that hazy land between sleeping and waking, and try to remember where I am. Keeping my eyes closed, I listen for clues. The *ding ding ding* sound of a soft bell brings it all back. I am in hospital.

This realization depresses me. I want to go back to sleep.

"Missus Dawson. Missus Dawson. Good morning Missus Dawson…it's a new day." The nurse's voice, feigning a cheery note, disturbs my reverie. I refuse to open my eyes.

"Come now, Missus Dawson, time for your pain medication…and then breakfast will be here in a moment."

I ignore her sickening Pollyanna happiness. She persists. Which tired nurse is it this time….Susan or Myrtle or Janet … *who cares who?* I've been here too long. Time to go home.

"Oh there you are, Missus Dawson. Bright as a button. I'll just raise your bed….." It is Susan and she blathers on as I reluctantly open my right eye. Sometimes my left eyelid stays closed of its own accord, as if it has a mind of its own.

"Today," she smiles too brightly, "is the day you get tested in the kitchen to see whether you can go back home." She pauses, looking at me. "I bet you pass. Why, you're getting to be as spry as a young chicken." What liars these nurses are. Susan is patting my sheets, plumping my pillows, chattering to me as if I am a child.

I am not a child. I am an 80-year-old woman with her faculties intact and I've had one hell of an active life and staying in the institutional wing of this hospital is a fate I will fight against despite the wishes of my damn family.

Imagine! I'm being tested to see whether I can cook in the kitchen of this place. Can I boil water? Can I safely use the kettle? Can I make a simple meal? All this so I can earn my stars to go home where I can live the way I want to. I hate these bitches they call nurses.

Me. Cecilia Dawson. Known far and wide for her hospitality, her gourmet meals, her generosity to all who come to her table.

Me. Cecilia Dawson. Mother of four, two of whom, are, unfortunately, questionable citizens. One has gone off the deep end mentally and I keep trying to stop blaming myself. What's that Erma Bombeck, my favourite now dead columnist, once said? 'Guilt is the gift that keeps on giving'. It wasn't my fault my daughter got mixed up in drugs and decided to be a drag on society and her family. Another kid turned out gay. Dan, my deceased husband --- God rest his soul --- and I did lots of research on that one and couldn't figure out where the gay bit came in. This son just disappeared. Left the house at 19 and never came back. We think he's still alive somewhere but don't know. Never heard from him again.

Ah, but Bernadette and Josie…they are my pride and joy. A bit misguided these days it seems. Thinking I need help at home or else they'll worry about me. Nonsense. Nothing is wrong with me that a good manhattan won't fix. A bit of this favourite libation is all I need. These meds I'm on are no good. One keeps me up. The other keeps me down. One makes me pee. The other makes me constipated. Quite frankly, I told Dr. Wayling, if everyone left my body alone I'd be a lot better off. Don't trust the medical profession these days. I've researched on my own and gone the alternative route. That's why I've been in such good shape all these years.

My body doesn't look like my body at all right now. I was always a sexy little lady. I could give a great blow job and have an orgasm at the same time. Sex, how I loved it. Still do. But all this medication is messing me up.

My hair may be grey at the roots but it's cut in a short bob, rather stylish. Soon's I get outa here, I'm heading for my favourite hairdresser, Guy. My Guy is gay but that's okay. He loves my clear blue eyes. Well, they *were* clear before I fell and came in here and took all this medication I should not take. It would be easy to just give up. My skin isn't bad. Not too wrinkled because I spent a fortune on Laroche Posay products with all that Vitamin C to keep my face smooth and soft.

Worked, too. Then when I switched to organic, the wrinkles just stopped altogether. A bit saggy I am but hey…for my age I'm eye candy for any man in his seventies. Most of these old geezers can't get it up anyway. What I need is a howling good orgasm but how the hell am I going to get that? As the Rolling Stones belted out long ago: *Can't Get No Satisfaction.*

It's time to get out of here but can't get no satisfaction in that department either. I'll be a good girl and do what they say so I can get out. No way Bernie and Josie are keeping me in here. I can cook. I can wash and dry dishes. I can turn the stove off and on. I can pee. I can walk and talk. I want out of this jail.

What's that Susan is saying?

"… Dr. Wayling will be in this morning. He'll want to take a good look at you. It's up to him whether you have to stay longer or not." She smiles in that sickeningly professional way as if she already knows what's going to happen but she knows I don't so she thinks she has some power over me.

A sad little creature from the corridor carries a food tray over to my bed. She looks like she should be the one in bed, not me. I eye her suspiciously as she places the tray on the bedside trolley. Little stainless steel tops cover the hidden food sitting on the 'property of Edgewood Hospital' dishes. As if we are in a high class restaurant. Ha! This place has no idea what good food is. I've been all over the world and eaten in some mighty grand places and tasted some gastronomic delights. I sniff at the breakfast tray and stare my nastiest glare at the sad little creature who timidly backs out of my private room.

"Well," says Susan, "are we going to eat? Or are we going to be difficult?" How I hate that *we* bit.

I lift the metal cover off my egg cup and look at the little brown oval. I asked for hard boiled but it's probably soft. Which means the yolk will run all over the plate and into my toast. I hate runny eggs. I like everything nice and tidy. Everything in its place, please. So, is this what my life has come to? Lying in a hospital bed hoping to get back to my own home?

Perhaps I'm lucky they never discovered I am a murderer.

You think I'm kidding? Well, I'm not.

It was back 50 years---half a century ago!--- when I was having this bizarre affair. I must have been crazy, but I felt alive and tingly and I loved the sensation of illicit meetings and liaisons. The chemistry between Bill and me sizzled with excitement at first. I could hardly wait for Dan to leave for work then I'd call Bill next door on some pretence or other, like the sink needed fixing or the couch needed moving, and over he'd come, like a panting dog. He knew he was in for a fucking good time.

It was just a diversion, you know? I'd always been what they call a 'good' girl, and suddenly I just didn't feel like being good anymore, you know what I mean? And there was tall, gangly Bill with those brown puppy dog eyes that followed me wherever I went. Those hungry eyes shot up and down my ripe body. I had pretty good breasts in those days and he couldn't have been more obvious about wanting to touch and milk them. He just had that desperate look; there was always a wet spot on his pants between his legs and I loved teasing him about it.

His wife, Doris, was a sweet, hard-working office-type person. But totally boring. I bet they didn't play in bed. In fact, I bet they wore pyjamas. Imagine! Dan and I never wore any night clothes and because of that we had four children, I swear. Nothing like the feel of bare skin to bare skin. Kind of wakes you up no matter what sleepy state you're in.

Bill and I made love everywhere in my house. I'd come up behind him in the bathroom while he was trying to fix a pipe and rub his crotch. "Now, Cec," he'd say, "at least let me finish what you called me for." I always ignored him. I'd touch his crotch again and his cock would spring into action.

"Dammit, Cec," he'd say. "When are we going to cut the games and divorce our partners and get together? Sometimes when I see you with Dan I go crazy with jealousy."

Silly Billy. Like all men, he thought with his cock. No way I wanted to give up Dan for Bill. Dan was far superior. He provided a good life; we had begun to travel; and more than that, Dan was a damn good lay. Bill was like a change, you know? I couldn't see myself living with Bill at all. I didn't like his personal habits----he had dirty fingernails for instance---and once I saw his underwear wasn't spanking clean that grossed me out. No, I'd never give up Dan for Bill but stupid Bill couldn't see that. Did he think we'd fuck everywhere if we got together? Not likely. He couldn't seem to realize it was the novelty, the spontaneity of the trysts that kept this affair going. He was no prize catch.

Eventually Bill became a problem, as most men do when it comes to sex. He was beginning to find excuses to come to the house----I wasn't calling him over---and he was beginning to think I was his, which led to some controlling behaviour. That's when I realized this little adventure had to end. Bill was far too possessive and to be honest, it scared me a little.

I tried to cool it naturally. "Bill, let's not see each other for a while. It's more exciting to be with each other after a break. So let's try that approach."

That didn't last a week. He was over after three days, with that poor-me look. He was in rutting season and didn't take too kindly at being brushed off. As far as he was concerned, I was his during daylight hours. As a night watchman, he could sleep on the job for awhile without any fear of repercussion. He had it all worked out with a buddy system.

Truthfully, Bill was becoming a drag. I had created a monster that wouldn't go away. When he was with me, I'd try and talk some sense into him but all he did was reach for my clothes to tear them off.

He also had a violent temper, I soon discovered, when he didn't get his way. If I didn't succumb to his charms, he'd get ugly. He sank to prepubescent behaviour. Like kicking the tires of my car. Not once but three or four times. Viciously. Or attacking my car with a key. Once he destroyed my front garden by fiercely stomping on those innocent flowers. I worried about being his next victim.

One especially vexing day, I took the bull by the horns and told him I wanted to end the whole thing. No more seeing him. No more sex. I was even thinking of telling his wife, which would have severe consequences.

"You do that, Cec, and I'll make damn sure Dan knows everything, too. He'll know it's true when I tell him where he puts his slippers at night and what drawers are his and where he keeps his beer and....."

"Shut up, Bill," I said. "This isn't going to work. I just want you to cool your jets for a while."

"So Miss High and Mighty wants everything her way," he said. "Well, this can get pretty messy if you want."

I hid my fear. "Get out of here, Bill. Go back to your own house. I'll rattle your cage when I want you."

Glaring at me with narrow sinister eyes, I could tell he was practicing full self-control by not hitting me. Enraged, he turned and stormed away.

Each time I left the house after that confrontation, Bill followed me. If I was driving, he was right behind me. If I was walking, he was behind me about a block. He was forever calling on the phone so I stopped answering. He'd begin his conversation the same way each time: *"so what are you doing now? I'm waiting to come over. I can see into your bedroom window. Imagine us in your bed. Together. Fucking...."* He always talked dirty. Turned him on and thought it turned me on, too. At first, yes, but now, no. After a few of these unwelcome calls, I began scheming to get rid of him.

The best way, I decided, was a medical emergency. A natural heart attack would be best but highly unlikely. As far as I knew he was as healthy as a horse, no heart problems. I couldn't just murder him... I wasn't the type. Besides, I didn't want to spend the rest of my life in prison.

So I began to think creatively. Ever since I told him we should cool it, Bill had become a stalker. In fact, I swear I saw him one night in the bushes outside our bedroom window. Even

Dan mentioned he thought he saw someone in the backyard. That terrified me, really. Bill was too aggressive and again, I feared for my personal safety. Once, when we were talking, I asked him if he had gone into our backyard. He was almost proud of his antics. *"Sure my sweet lady. It's a challenge to see how often I can spy on you without you seeing me. A neat game. Saw you ruffle Dan's hair the other night when he was sittin' in the living room and I damned near knocked out the window I was so jealous. What d'ya figure he might have said if I did that? If he asked me what I was doing I'd tell him the truth. That you and me's bin pretty hot and heavy lately and so what did he expect when I saw you runnin' your hands through his hair. What d'ya suppose Dan would say, sweet girl? Would he be surprised? Hurt? Wonderin' if I was telling the truth? Huh? Well, what d'ya think, sweet lady?"*

That diatribe did it. I vowed to get rid of this dickhead. Fast. And forever.

After some musing, the solution came to me. If I could get Bill to run a red light or something -- get involved in a car accident -- then maybe he'd get really injured and leave me alone.

I thought about this strategy for a while. First, I tested it. Yep, each time I left the house in my car, Bill was right behind me. I had to find a place and time to set up a car accident. This became my prime focus and motivation. No-one else should get hurt either. This agitated state was between Bill and me. I had gotten myself into this mess and had to get myself out of it.

The first attempt at a car accident failed. Like I expected, he drove on my tail. A man obsessed. I stopped at a stop sign. Looked both ways. A red car was approaching on my left. Figured there was enough time for one, but not two, cars to make it across the intersection. Gunned the accelerator, shot across the street, and could hear the squealing brakes of the red car. Looked in the rear view mirror. Like an idiot, Bill spurted right after me. Almost gave *me* a heart attack but no accident.

After that, I was determined to get rid of this leech forever--- and soon. There was a railroad crossing not far from the edge of town. I was sure it did not have car barriers. If I could time it to drive just in front of an oncoming train and Bill was intent on following me... well, I could get lucky and Bill, well, maybe not so lucky. So I called the train station and asked about timing at scheduled train crossings.

On the morning I prepared to carry out my plan, I was a little edgy. You could say, excited. The adrenalin was running. I carefully went over the route in my mind so I'd be at the railroad crossing the last possible moment to get myself over the tracks.

Driving to the scene of the crime, I could hear the train whistle in the distance. I could see the wigwags beginning to clack and red lights flash back and forth. As I approached the crossing I glanced behind. Yep, Bill was there. Not too close but he was there. Actually, he was moving closer and closer as I reached the crossing and was almost on me.

I had to time this perfectly. The train whistle blew longer, louder. Gunning the car just before the train bore down on the crossing, I prayed. Right behind me, I could see Bill gunning his car....

Bill's funeral was a sad affair for many---he would have loved the wonderful accolades people gave him---but I felt sorry for Doris. Eventually she would go on to find someone new and that was good. Bill really wasn't right for her. As for me, I felt only a sense of grateful relief.

"Missus Dawson?" queries nurse Susan dragging me back to the present. "Why, you haven't touched your breakfast tray! You won't be allowed to leave the hospital until you prove you're healthy enough. I'll have to report this to Dr. Wayling."

"Susan," I snarl, "how'd you like to get smashed to smithereens at a railroad crossing by a fast-moving train?"

"Oh," she smiles sweetly looking down at me, "is that how you got rid of my Uncle Bill?"

-- Semi-finalist; John Kenneth Galbraith Award 2014

-- Pick of the Day, CommuterLit 2015

The Caller

Her smartphone rings as she carefully applies her black mascara. Running late that morning, Deanna impatiently reaches for it on the bathroom vanity.

"Hello," she snaps.

Dead. Another hang up.

For a moment she frowns and stares at the phone, then touches the caller ID button. While she doesn't recognize the number, she does notice it isn't the first time this caller has called. She needs to find time to investigate and see who is bugging her. Over the past weeks this mystery caller has called a few times a day, then hangs up as soon as she answers. A wrong number? She doesn't think so and is beginning to feel uncomfortable.

A marketing executive, Deanna is on the fast track to a new position overseas with her international company. She has worked hard, played hard, tried very hard not to get involved in office politics or office romances and feels completely in control of her life. Except lately. This unwelcome caller is unnerving her and she needs to put an end to it.

As she sweeps through the corridors of the high-rise concrete tower on the way to her corner office, Deanna is herself again. Attractive, but not beautiful, she's taken advantage of her physical assets: an hour-glass figure, brunette shoulder length hair glowing with golden highlights, full lips like Angelina Jolie's, a sultry voice, and the ability to articulate her thoughts without ending her sentences in a question, as so many of those young dense initiates do. "I believe this is going to be a good idea?" they'll query. How many times has Deanna taken Lilly aside to educate her? "You do NOT say *I believe*, Lilly. You say ***This is*** *going to be a good idea.* Period. Not a question. Sound like you know what you're talking about even if you don't. And stop cocking your head like a bird. You're knowledgeable so show it. Don't act like some dumb broad."

It incenses Deanna when young women think playing coy is the best way to get ahead. Not in this male dominated company, she warns them. Be assertive. Speak with authority. Go into that meeting and spread your papers and files all over the table so the guys know they are dealing with someone who is confident.

With that last thought she removes the report from her briefcase, walks with a controlled but feminine gait down the hall, flings open the board room door and looks around at her male counterparts. She is third---the only female---of eight senior administrators to arrive at the meeting.

"Yo Deanna," salutes Ted raising his forefinger from across the mahogany table. Deanna acknowledges his greeting with a warm smile and nod.

A weird thought suddenly strikes her. *Is it him? Could Ted be the one who is calling her anonymously?* They are both in running for the overseas posting but she knows Ted isn't interested. His wife doesn't want to leave Toronto; she is one of the city's movers and shakers. No way would she play second fiddle to Ted's career. Besides, Ted isn't exactly a prime representative for the company. He can't speak German while she can and he is a sloppy dresser while she is tailored by Holt Renfrew.

She turns her attention to Brian. Solid, conservative in thinking and dress, Brian just doesn't seem the type to harass her. Besides, his wife would kill him. He is brow-beaten.

Benjamin strides boldly into the room just then. Good-looking. Suave. Twice-divorced and a ladies' man. Both have locked horns over several marketing campaigns and although Deanna eventually got her way with gentle persuasion, Brian was professional enough not to hold it against her. Or was he?

Why, all of a sudden, does she think it is one of these upper echelon men who is harassing her? Just as quickly she realizes her overactive imagination is getting out of hand.

At noon the meeting breaks for a working lunch. People reach for their cell phones and begin to sift through messages.

Deanna's phone rings, too. She immediately sees the mystery caller---*private number*---on the display screen. Quickly, she glances around the room. Not one of her seven colleagues could possibly be the intruder; each is intimately involved in some high-powered conversation. Even though she knows the outcome, she answers. Another dead call.

Because of this phantom caller, Deanna feels a vague threat to her well-ordered life. After the long business meeting, she starts thinking seriously about who might want to antagonize her. This mysterious harasser has found her Achilles heel, for Deanna's passion in life is being in complete control.

Back in her office, she stares at her co-workers. Is it that creep over by the window who's always leering at her? Is it one of the girls she is trying to mentor, like Lilly? Is it the guy in the elevator who always smirks when they happen to enter at the same time? Is it the cleaning woman who can see all her contact info on her desk? Good grief, girl, get a grip, she scolds herself.

"I can't understand it," she mentions to her best friend Ruth at the gym after work. It is 8 p.m. and the mystery caller is beginning to occupy her mind after work.

"Oh, you probably have some secret admirer who's afraid to approach you because you're so powerful and unattainable. Trace the call. It's easy enough to do."

"You're right of course. Except you won't believe I haven't had a chance I've been so busy. I could just reply to the number. But then what?"

"Well, you just might find out who the caller is."

"But what if I don't like the answer to that question?"

"Then you've got a problem, Dee. Just be sure you don't get involved with someone unsavoury. You know the weird stories you hear about dysfunctional types out there."

Back outside her home in the gathering darkness, Deanna slowly unlocks the door to her midtown Victorian duplex. Some instinct cautions her to look around, check that no-one is watching. Is there someone lurking in the shadows by the bushes? She sees friendly lights in the windows of the Holden house across the street and shakes herself back to reality. Their four teenage kids come and go all hours of the day and night. She feels safe and not quite as vulnerable with them so close.

Once inside, she quickly turns on all the lights, locks the door behind her and feels comfort in the *beep beep beep* of the security system that she immediately disengages. Misty, her beloved pet, comes running to greet her, pressing against her leg for attention. She picks up the Siamese, stroking her softly and closes the venetian blinds. Misty purrs.

"I'm going crazy, little one," she mewls into the cat's ear. Misty cocks her head and stares with crystal blue eyes at Deanna. "Me. Can you imagine? Confident, independent me. I've got to stop this person intruding in my life."

Gently putting her pet down, she walks to the cupboard to open Misty's nightly Natural Balance meal treat, and then sits down staring at her cell. She scrolls down the list of archived calls and finds the mystery number she wanted. Dare she call it?

She does.

The phone rings and rings. No message machine. Nothing.

Turning on her computer, she clicks to 411.ca and tries a reverse look-up. Nothing.

Uneasy, Deanna turns on the television just for background noise. CBC News is airing a special, coincidentally on stalking. She sits down, drawn to the program like a magnet. She does not like what she sees or hears. Reporting her anonymous calls to the police does not seem like a plausible idea at this time since they are just hang-ups. No threats. No talk. Probably from a payphone. She doesn't want to come across as hysterical or start some sort of investigation within the company. Should she enlist HR for help? What about EAP, the Employee Assistance Program?   That kind of notation might put chances for a foreign transfer in jeopardy.   Maybe she'll call the telephone company in the morning.   But that will have to wait.   She has to be in the office for an overseas conference call by 6 a.m.   Lots of prep work needed.   It is time for common sense to prevail, she chides herself.

Not knowing why, Deanna brings her cell into the bathroom placing it on the vanity while she sinks into the tub. Luxuriating in the bubbles of Jason's Natural Foam bath cream, she muses about her life and how far she has come from the small-town girl who first came to the big city.

Many of Deanna's friends can't understand why she is still single.   She certainly does not lack sensuality and they could not know Deanna favours women for partners.   Long ago in Renfrew she had fallen in love with Lorraine, a willowy black-haired beauty with alabaster skin.   Lorraine was one year ahead of her in high school and Deanna actually froze in her presence she was so love-struck.   A golden glow surrounded Lorraine and Deanna caught her breath whenever they were together. Nothing physical happened between them despite a mutual attraction and Deanna remained forever in awe of Lorraine's grace and talents.   As far as Deanna is concerned this kind of love is pure and uncomplicated, not like messy relationships with guys.   So she clings to this romantic ideal and never bothers with anyone else.   She tried looking for Lorraine during reunions, googling her name, asking people about her.   Now that she is a confident businesswoman, she wonders whether she would be more attractive to Lorraine.   So far her search for Lorraine remains unsuccessful.   "Probably married with a dozen kids," says sensible Ruth.   The fact this could be true bothers Deanna who now prefers Lorraine on an imaginary pedestal, unchanged from her high school days.

Over the next weeks Deanna is constantly on edge.   Sporadic phone hang ups, all from different numbers leave her jittery, unusual Dee behaviour quickly noticed around the office.

"Big date tonight?" teases Ted.   "Can't concentrate?"

"You're awfully high strung these days, Big Dee," says Brian.

"Well, look who's getting antsy," taunts Benjamin. "Maybe we otta go for a drink after work, Dee."

At the gym, even Ruth notices. "What's the matter, Dee?"

Deanna starts to explain when her phone rings. Automatically her heart starts racing. She stares at the unfamiliar number.

"Hello."

 No answer. Just another hang-up like dozens of others.

"Is that jerk still bothering you? Do something about it, silly. I can see it's driving you nuts."

Why bother telling Ruth the harasser is now using different numbers? Each hang-up just sets her on edge again. She glances suspiciously around the locker room.

That evening, as she is unlocking the door to her home, hurried footsteps from behind make her wheel around in fright.

"Deanna," frowns Mrs. Holden touching her arm. "Listen, something terrible has happened. Somehow Misty got out of the house today and ......" she pauses.

"And what?" Deanna asks, her mind trying to absorb the fact Misty had actually gotten out. She was a house cat and never left home.

"Well, a car... a car hit her."

"What!?"

"A car hit her. One of our boys rushed her to the animal hospital. Oh, I'm so sorry to have to tell you this..."

Only then the magnitude of what happened to her beloved pet begins to register. "What!? Where!?" She frowns, not able to think straight.

By the time Deanna gets to the vet, Misty has died. Traumatized, Deanna is crushed. She can't believe Misty is gone. She can't believe Misty had gotten out of the house on her own. Bad thoughts keep tumbling on and on. First, some creep is driving her crazy with calls and now this, the worst possible news. She can't believe all these things are happening to her. Misty, who pranced to the door each morning and greeted her at the door each evening, was her only family. She slept with Misty. Her soul was intertwined with Misty as much as any pet lover's would. Tears flow as misery, shock and horror shake her very core.

When she finally returns home for the second time that night, she stands at the door looking at it as if for the first time. Somehow her home no longer represents security; it gives rise to suspicion and fear. Carefully she inserts her key in the lock and opens the door. The first thing that raises a red flag is not hearing the familiar *beep beep beep* of the security system. Something isn't right.

Stunned she begins to walk through the house. How had Misty escaped? Had she left open a window? Impossible. Deanna always checked the windows every night and every morning. Misty would not leave unless someone forced her out.

With that sinister thought, Deanna feels the hairs rise on the back of her neck. Her confidence melts and her legs are like globs of gelatin.

Slowly, carefully, she begins to search her house. She turns on lights as she enters each room. Nothing suspicious in the kitchen or living room on the main floor. She checks the balcony. Nothing out of the ordinary. The patio table is still there waiting to be painted and the chairs are exactly as she left them the night before.

Stealthily she moves to the second-floor landing. There is that one creaking board on the hardwood floor reminding her she must get it repaired before it drives her crazy. Gingerly, she checks the guest room and adjoining bathroom. Nothing out of place. She peers cautiously into the den. The computer still sits there waiting for her. A walk around the room shows everything in place.

Finally she moves to her haven, her bedroom with the ensuite bath. As she slowly checks everything out, she begins to sigh with relief. At the same time tears roll down her cheeks as she thinks about Misty.

A bath would be good for her tonight. A relaxing bubble bath and a slug of Southern Comfort to get her through the emotional pain. She needs to calm down, to think clearly and decide her next move.

Carefully placing her cell on the vanity praying it would not ring, she submerges her exhausted body into the warm water. Only then did the damn phone start ringing. Again and again. Over and over. Driving her crazy. Finally the ringing stops. But what is that strange sound? Straining her ears, without moving a muscle, without drawing a breath, she listens. Horrified, she hears the squeak of the loose floorboard. Someone is in her home! Emerging panic-stricken from the bath water, she reaches for her cell. At the same time, an unknown hand clamps hard over her mouth, another hand yanks her hair from behind throwing her cell into the bath water. Then the lights go out. Deanna is no longer in control.

2^(nd) place, CAA, Niagara Branch, 2014

Judge's comments: The Caller - "Taut, well-paced and immediately involving, 'The Caller' is reminiscent of suspense masters such as Patricia Highsmith. The disruption of a normal, workaday life by an unseen threat (or is the threat merely imagined?) invites us into a distinctly contemporary world of paranoia, the anxieties of invaded privacy taken to a nightmarish level" - Andrew Piper, well known writer of 6 novels including the national bestseller Demonologist

Pandora's Box

She discovered the affair because of her insomnia. On that night, unable to sleep--- again---Jen rose quietly from their bed in the dim light of the bedroom.

Glancing at her sleeping husband, she tiptoed to the window and peeked between the slats of the venetian blinds.

That's when she saw Josef Demetrios, who lived in the condo across the street with his wife and teenage son, look furtively around him in the moonlight as he carefully stepped down his porch, still glancing this way and that.

Hidden from view behind the blinds, Jen watched him, fascinated. Josef was one of those charming, good-looking Greek immigrants with a continental style and easy-going manner. She admitted to herself she could easily picture him between the sheets of her bed. Smiling to herself, she glanced at Ted who slept like an angel now but who had been guilty of adultery many years ago.

She saw Josef moving swiftly now. To Jen's surprise, he turned into the condo next to him. She watched as the door opened and he slipped inside quickly. Her neighbour, Cecilia, a single mom of two primary school children, had obviously been waiting for him. She watched to see if a light went on in Cecilia's home. There was none.

Jen moved away from the window, silently descended the carpeted staircase with the one squeaky step and slid into the kitchen. Maybe a Black Russian, her favourite comfort drink of vodka and Kahlua, would help her sleep. Gliding into the living room with her glass and sinking into Ted's swivel chair, she pulled out a Benson and Hedges, lit it, and savoured the first inhale. Then she took her first sip.

Alone in Ted's favourite chair, her hands cupped around her drink, and fresh from the discovery of deceit she had just witnessed, memories flooded back to her over her husband's affair. How had she discovered it? She frowned while she was thinking and looked around the familiar room furnished in Scandinavian furniture accented with dashes of burgundy and blue cushions set off by a circular, multi-coloured area carpet. She was not an interior decorator but knew she had an eye for design.

Facing her was the Greek mythological tapestry she and Ted had purchased together at least 30 years ago in Athens. It showed the beautiful Pandora, who, on an order from Zeus, was fashioned from clay and water and designed to drive men crazy. Pandora was blithely opening her jar that was filled with the terrible afflictions of mankind: ills, toils, and sickness. These awful maladies immediately escaped and spread over the world. Only Hope did not fly away. And so, according to legend, misery made its first appearance on earth with the arrival of Pandora, the first woman.

Jen stubbed out her cigarette and pensively stared at the tapestry again, as if for the first time. She could recall the little shopkeeper on the side street in Plaka watching as she and Ted, holding hands and very much in love, perused the artifacts of his store. They couldn't decide between the tapestry or a terra cotta vase adorned with the Amazons but finally chose the tapestry because it was easier to pack.

Jen sipped her Black Russian, lifting it to the ambient light long enough to appreciate the shade of the drink's seductive chocolate. She had met Ted in a continuing education class of Greek mythology at Sheridan College in Toronto. They shared a passion for all things Greek. Their first date was at the Mykonos Grill in the Danforth area where they shared a bottle of red kouros and he told her he thought she had the most beautiful blue eyes, the colour of the Aegean Sea. Her golden hair, he said, was the colour of waving wheat fields in the Canadian prairies.

And what did she say to him on that faraway night? Jen knit her brows together, slowly sipping her drink and lighting another cigarette. She was awestruck and flattered this young and handsome financial wizard with the dark eyes and black wavy hair was sitting across the table holding her hand over the white linen tablecloth.

Stretching back in time, Jen couldn't remember what they had to eat except for the flaming saganaki with the obligatory Opa! but she did remember the waiters hanging around hoping they would leave as the minutes flew into hours and the hours stretched into a night of wild love-making and then watching the sunrise together over Toronto's Harbourfront.

What had happened since then between them? When did it turn sour? Was she too busy? Was he? Two children, a precious boy and a flaxen haired girl within three years, hadn't helped their romance. She was far too tired all the time. When the children were old enough, she went back to selling pharmaceuticals while Ted steadily rose in the corporate ranks of an international company. Her job brought business travel opportunities. Over the years in lonely hotel rooms, she certainly had plenty of chances to cheat. But she didn't. She couldn't face their children if she betrayed their father.

But Ted? There had been Alta, his exotic personal assistant originally from Lebanon. "Oh, please, Mr. Ted, show me the ways of Canada!" she purred. One day Jen received an anonymous telephone call telling her it might be in her best interests to hire a private detective to follow her husband. She was sick to her stomach after that call. She knew there were other dalliances, too, and couldn't understand why Ted stayed with her. For the children who were now adults and living their own lives? Jen scoffed. Who knew the inner thoughts of a philandering husband? For her own part, why did she stay with Ted? Was it familiarity? Too much trouble to divorce? Not getting any younger?

She shrugged. She and Ted seemed to have fallen into a pattern of living together without really living together--- except when the children came home to visit.

Her thoughts turned back to her neighbours, Cecilia and Josef. She hoped they knew what they were risking. Brushing a blonde curl from her now drowsy eyes, she tiptoed back into her bedroom. Before she slid between the sheets, she peeked out between the slats. Nothing. All was dark. She had just happened to see something she shouldn't have.

Her last thought before settling down again was that Cecilia was single so had every right to engage in a relationship, however illicit, with whomever she pleased. It was the dark-haired handsome Greek who stood the most to lose. Cecilia thought briefly about Josef's quiet and dutiful wife, Maria, who seemed to adore her wanderlust husband.

In the rush of getting ready for work the next morning, as she gulped her instant Maxwell House coffee and munched a tasteless store-bought carrot muffin, Jen's mind jumped back to last night and the forbidden scene across the street. And then she was lost in the day's events.

After dinner, because she was out of cigarettes, she walked to the corner 7-11. Pretending to walk for exercise, she knew she wasn't fooling herself. She needed her Benson and Hedges fix. On the other side of the store, looking over the movie titles, she was sure she recognized Maria.

"Maria?" she said tentatively.

Josef's diminutive wife whirled around.

"Hello, Jen," she said, in a warm European accent. "So nice to see you. I never really see you since you work all day."

Jen nodded. "It's true." Then looking at the shelf she asked, "Looking for a good movie?"

Maria nodded. "Hmmmm. Josef and I love to watch them late into the night. Trouble is I usually fall asleep while it's still running. You'd think I worked all day like you."

Jen paused, wondering what to say next.

"Um, Maria, how is Josef able to watch late movies and then get up so early for work the next day? He mustn't need much sleep."

Maria smiled demurely. "He is amazing that man of mine. Sometimes when I wake up in the middle of the night and he's not there, I know he's downstairs working in the den."

"Really?" said Jen curiously. She paused, bit her lip. "By the way, how's Damien?"

"Oh, you know teenagers, especially boys. Sometimes he's in early and sometimes he's in late. I can't keep track of him."

Jen changed her tack. "How is Cecilia….you know…your neighbour? I was wondering how she was making out being a single mom and all. Do you know? I think she's absolutely amazing."

Maria beamed. "Both Josef and Damien help her out with household chores…you know, a leaky tap, a squeaky door. She really appreciates it. And your husband is good with her, too. I don't know what Cecilia would do without our men!" Smiling, she turned back to the movie selections.

Jen stood there in shock. Did Maria just say that Ted was with Cecilia? When could he possibly have time? Certainly he was in bed beside her every night. In one split second Jen's mind began jumping in a million directions. Ted? How could he? After the humiliation and heartache and trying to forgive his other indiscretions he was at it again? But how? And when?

She looked at the seemingly serene Maria perusing the movie titles and opened her mouth to speak. She wanted to ask Maria all sorts of questions. But she also didn't want to appear as if she didn't know what her own husband was doing.

Instead, Jen snapped her mouth shut, turned around and walked out the store, dimly aware she was doing all this but not concentrating on the moment at all.

As soon as she got home, she slumped into the rattan chair on the back patio and lit a cigarette. Watching the smoke spiral upwards she felt that old pang of panic, of betrayal, once more. *That sick in the pit of my stomach feeling.*

She glanced at her watch: 7:00 p.m. They had finished dinner an hour ago. Ted said he was going for a walk while she slipped down to the 7-11 for cigarettes. Where the hell was he? Why didn't she go with him on that walk? Old fears, insecurities, abandonment issues welled up inside her.

Suddenly the haunting memories of her troubled marriage rushed back to her. The therapist took a long time to get to the real issue. Or maybe he deliberately took a long time just so he could make more money. Jen shut her eyes for a minute. She was so suspicious of everyone. So critical. So jaded with life. Maybe that was her real problem and not that she hated sex.

Sex to Jen was always distasteful. And ridiculous, really. She snorted through her smoky nose. Imagine Ted's feet in the air as he contorted his body, trying to penetrate her from different directions. What ridiculous postures, she thought. She tried to enjoy sex. Really, she thought. She tried to thaw out. She drank to relax during sex. Didn't work. All she got was tired. She tried to imagine a hot hunk pumping into her. Didn't work. She could have cared less. She tried therapy. Didn't work. Whatever the problem was in their love-making, it was hers.

She was grateful when she was pregnant. A perfect excuse for no sex for a long time. And then she landed her demanding job. A perfect cover: always tired.

She stubbed out her cigarette as she heard the front door slam.

"Ted?" she demanded.

"Yep."

"Where were you?" She tried to sound casual, nonchalant, totally uncaring.

A long pause.

"I was over helping Cecilia fix her bicycle seat." Another pause. "She couldn't loosen the bolt so she asked for some help." Ted was beside her now.

"I see you're smoking as usual." His tone was not pleasant.

"Of course," she said. "Do you see Cecilia often when I'm not around?" *Damn. Damn. Damn. She didn't mean to ask that. She didn't want the old fears to spill out so quickly.*

He frowned. "What the hell's that supposed to mean?"

"Sorry. Sorry," Jen apologized. "Don't know why I said that." Although she knew very well why she did. Suddenly she stood up and looked into his dark eyes. "I'm going in to do some work now." She deliberately stepped around him on her way inside.

That night, the same old problem. Unable to sleep, Jen tossed and turned before deciding to get up again. She glanced at the digital dial on the clock radio: 2 a.m. She had been a fool to get so uptight about Cecilia. But what the devil did Maria mean by her casual comment, *"And your husband is good with her, too."* What is the matter with me, she pondered. Why am I so paranoid? Why am I so jealous when I don't want to have anything physical to do with Ted anyway? What's my problem?

Out of habit, she peeked again through the blind slats onto the darkened street. Nothing. No activity tonight. Just as she was about to turn away, she saw a dark shadow flip down the steps of the condo across the way. She focused closer, wondering how Josef could keep up these nightly visits to his mistress and remain alert the next day at his insurance firm. Maybe she should sit Maria down and tell her the facts of life regarding her handsome husband.

Still watching, Jen saw Josef quickly cross to the next door condo and disappear quickly into the open door, obviously into the arms of Cecilia. Damn husband, thought Jen. What a mess husbands and wives can make of their lives.

Now her mind was working overtime. Surely Maria must know what Josef is up to. Jen certainly knew. Maybe she doesn't care, thought Jen. Maybe she's like me and is quite happy to have Josef as her husband but not as her lover.

Jen shook her blonde tousled head of hair and sighed. She was amazed at what was going on after hours in this quiet suburban neighbourhood. Twisting her mouth, she thought about the TV series *Desperate Housewives*. But who was desperate? How did Cecilia find the energy? Was she as sexually starved as Jen imagined or was she really interested in baiting and trapping a mate, no matter whose husband it was? Men are such fools, she thought. They think with their cocks and not their heads. Not an original thought she reminded herself but nevertheless, a true one. The Black Russian and a Benson and Hedges soothed her soul and once again she felt the peace of sleep slowly begin to sweep over her.

Over the next weeks, Jen watched the drama unfold across the darkened street. She almost looked forward to her night owl awakenings as if it was time for her soap opera.

Occasionally she thought about Maria. Perhaps, like the anonymous phone tip she once received, she should alert Maria to what was happening. If she accidentally bumped into her sometime, then she would hint at something. She didn't want to get involved but neither did she want Maria to continue blithely in darkness concerning the shapely Cecilia who was obviously comforting her husband.

And what about her own? She glanced at Ted, asleep as usual in their bed, and shook her head. When could he possibly be with Cecilia? Still, the germ of the idea had been planted and she couldn't shake it.

Back she went again to her past. Now she was a preteen, perhaps twelve years old, she thought. A happy, content girl, she remembers. Until that dark day she entered the town's general store. Old Mr. Sutherland, his girth as round as a seven-months-pregnant woman, was in the store that day. In her hot hand, Jen held a dime that was burning a hole in her pocket. She knew Sutherland's had a lot of penny candy.

The bell announcing customers jingled like a friend as she pushed open the decayed swinging door on this bright, hot July day. It took awhile for her eyes to get accustomed to the darkness of the interior. Finally she made out Mr. Sutherland who was always kind to her.

"Hi Jen," he beamed as she approached the counter. "What can I do for you?"

She glanced up and stared into his brilliantly blue eyes. Funny, she had never noticed how bright blue they were before. "Candy," she said simply.

"Come with me," he crooned. And he led her behind the counter---where no other child was allowed---and stood right behind her. "Choose whatever you want," he said. It took her a minute before she realized what he was doing. His big meaty hands were roving over her small budding breasts. She stopped moving. She hated to admit it but she sort of liked the feeling she got as he slowly rotated his hands over and around her small breasts. She felt a stirring down in the depths of her body between her legs.

"Do you like that?" he murmured softly. Jen didn't dare answer. She liked it but she didn't. It felt exciting but dirty and wrong. She just held her breath.

Now he led her back farther into the store, into the storage area, and turned around to face her. "Look," he said. And to Jen's disgust mixed with a strange lust, he took her hand and placed it around the huge erection of flesh that was pointing right at her. "Do touch it, Jen," purred Mr. Sutherland. "And you shall have all the candy you want. For free."

Suddenly the door bell jingled, Mr. Sutherland pulled up his zipper, and a shaken Jen was pulled back to reality...

It was a week night again when she peered, like a bad habit, between the blind slats and saw the familiar figure of Josef slipping silently down his condo stairs.

Josef was making his way across the lawn to Cecilia's when suddenly a blurred figure leapt from the bushes between the condos. Her eyes shot from one figure to the other and she gasped. Even in the dark she saw the silver glint of a knife blade. She saw the assailant's arm jerk up and down, up and down, over and over again.

Horrified, Jen slapped her hand across her mouth to silence her scream. She almost shook Ted awake to see what she was seeing. But Jen didn't do any of these things.

Instead, she quickly closed the blind slats. She stood behind the safety of the closed venetians and held her breath. She thought she heard moaning, a distant call for help, then silence. Dare she look, she thought?

No, she decided. She would not look. Her own life was complicated enough and she didn't want to get involved.

Instead, she took herself down to the kitchen, poured herself a large Black Russian, lit one of the Benson and Hedges and leaned back in Ted's swivel chair. The warmth of the Kahlua coated her throat and she sighed heavily, took a deep breath.

When she looked up, she saw the familiar Greek tapestry with the dazzlingly beautiful Pandora lifting the lid of her vase. As the siren wailing in the distance grew louder, she mused how the arrival of Pandora, the first woman, had unleashed misery over the earth.

- Semi-finalist, John Kenneth Galbraith Awards, 2009

Someone I Used to Know

Bounding with pizzazz across the stage in a tight bikini (*or was it a superb body paint job?*), she shook her bountiful breasts, wiggled her tight ass. Leaned provocatively over the lusting males in the first row.

On assignment for a small-town weekly (*you're a woman. Visit one of those sex shows. Interview one of their stars. Tell me how she got started. Why she's doing it. Any business angle, too, - make it titillating*), I watched, captivated. 'Raquel' strutted her stuff to a wild and crazy Calypso beat as multi-coloured strobe lights flashed around the club's dim interior. The smell of fried foods: greasy hamburgers, sizzling potatoes in oil-soaked wire baskets intermingled with the stench of stale beer, created an aura of debauchery.

Tossing her tangled platinum blonde mane like a wild beast, Raquel brazenly showed off her lithe body, with what looked like surgically enhanced breasts, in a jungle- patterned support bra and thong, moulded to her skin like a wet t-shirt.

It was hard to keep my eyes off her. Besides her stunning dance number, something about the turn of her neck, her face, her hands roaming up and down her curvaceous athletic body, was vaguely familiar. From my vantage point sitting in the back, she reminded me of someone. Fat chance any of my safe, staid friends would lead a double life like this!

As a journalist, my first instinct was to watch the crowd, see if they're engaged. Most were men but a sprinkling of women, all ages, studied the performer's every move. Before throwing her thong and bra into the audience, she seduced with her pole-dancing prowess. Her height on the gleaming pole led my eyes up, up to the dusty coils of a blackened pipe ceiling dotted with fake twinkling stars. Sliding provocatively back onstage, she locked eyes with a wealthy looking man in the front row. He was already reaching for his wallet.

I didn't notice the bar owner, Sweetheart Roxy, when she slipped into the booth beside me.

"Well," she said, "what d'ya think? She's our star." I nodded slowly. Despite the raucous music and fried fatty smells from the back kitchen, I continued concentrating on Raquel. She mesmerized me.

"Let's go to my office to discuss your article. I'd love the publicity. In fact, I need it!" Roxy chuckled. I instantly liked her: no pap. She was a slightly overweight former exotic dancer who still had to hold men at bay. 'Roxy's Room' was her business idea to make money when she could no longer collect her bucks on the dance floor.

"So, what's it like to be in the strip business in a lunch bucket town?"

She snorted. Lit a cigarette. "You mean an exotic dancer business, sweetheart," she corrected.

I smiled, nodded.

"For starters, sweetheart, this club is a bona fide business. I pay property taxes, employ security, hire fifteen dancers, some from around here. Our suppliers are local. Every product we use we try to buy in this area. A local photographer gets lots of business putting together the girls' portfolios. A local seamstress gets our business to sew exotic costumes..." She paused, that chuckle again, "'course, some costumes don't take much material." She laughed, deep and hearty. "What else you need to know, sweetheart?"

"Where do the girls learn their craft?"

"From me, mostly. They're clean green girls, students, housewives, who need money, are good looking, good bodies, healthy, willing to work hard during strange hours. Noon to midnight mostly. I warn 'em about drugs. Can't use 'em while they're with me. If they do, they're gone. No dating customers. At least not while I'm around. Do a lot of training cuz the working life of a dancer is very short. Oldest here is twenty-six. Youngest, eighteen. Feature dancer's usually from a big city.

Others do a short routine on stage but make their money as table dancers. They all own bling-bling costumes, with five-inch fuck me heels, and really strut their stuff. Flamboyant. Confident. Edgy. We give the customer what he wants."

She inhaled her cigarette, exhaled. Smoke drifted throughout the room. Her messy office reflected a jumbled state of mind: hodge-podge of piled papers in odd places. A computer, cell phone, printer, each competed for attention among the stacks on her desk. Stale smoke emanated from an overloaded ash tray. A half bottle of Absolut sat on the lone bookcase that held no books but lots of girlie photos. An out-of-date calendar with exotic dancer paintings hung above the bookcase. The sole window to an exterior alley was dressed in old-fashioned ivory lace curtains. Like grandma used to hang.

"So, still room for this sort of business to thrive?"

"Damn right, sweetheart. Exotic dancing has been around for centuries. Provides a service whether or not Suburban Wife thinks so. Get lots of businessmen in here on lunch hours. Could name a few well-knowners but we're discreet. Always." She dragged on her cigarette again, blew out the smoke. "Even Head of the Cop Shop comes in. Course, he says he's here on business -- our headliner was accused of stealing money from a regular -- but he coincidentally walked in just before her show so's he could watch." She snorted, blowing smoke rings to the ceiling. Winks.

"Would you say your dancers are exploited?"

She coughed, looked me in the eye. "They provide a service and are well paid for it. You call that exploitation?"

"I'd like to interview a dancer for this article."

Roxy lifted her brows. "Well, now, that depends. If the girl comes from around here, then no, you can't. One of the out-of-towners might take up your offer."

"Raquel....is she local?"

"Nope. From the east coast. And she won't be interviewed. Many have asked. None have succeeded."

"Okay if I ask her?"

Roxy looked me up and down. Shrugged. "You can ask but I'll tell you this. Raquel is one mysterious lady. She's experienced. Bin a feature dancer here a few weeks. Draws in the rich guys. But as soon as she's finished dancing, she disappears upstairs to her room. Tried to ask about her background but she's silent. Do know she's had body surgery. Nose, boobs. Somethin's happened in her past. Don't go messin' in places I don't belong. She brings in the customers and I'm happy. She gets paid well, gets left alone, she's happy."

I decided a one-time visit to Roxy's Room wasn't enough to grasp the complexity of this business, its patrons and clientele. I mean, maybe there's a place for this kind of entertainment after all. Better an oversexed guy comes here than grabs a female and rapes her. So I needed to return to digest this hormone-charged atmosphere… explore its heartbeat. Wanted time to think about the direction and format of the story. That was fine with Sweetheart Roxy.

Out in the sultry summer night heading for my car, I mulled over this centuries-old business. Sitting alone behind the steering wheel, my thoughts focused on Raquel, the headline dancer. She reminded me of someone I used to know, someone once very important to me: my first love at a summer camp when I was a teen. My heart and mind immediately slipped back to Silver Lake.

Never noticed Rachel -- or any girl for that matter -- until long after we were settled into our cabins and assigned duties as counsellors to young campers. We were hires from different city high schools after successfully completing wilderness training, grateful to land a summer position with the Y. Not working a boring job in the hot city as a sales clerk or fast-food order taker.

Busy during those first days settling our young campers, some homesick, some brats, some scared, others genuinely nice kids, I barely noticed my fellow counsellors.

Except Rachel. She immediately grabbed my attention. Was aware of her presence during meetings, camp activities, meals. Whenever I glanced her way, her eyes met mine. Eyes that captivated me because of their large pupils and unusual colour: violet. Like Elizabeth Taylor, the famous movie star.

Long and lithe in body, Rachel wore her short black hair in a pixie style that framed her oval face and showed off those exquisite violet eyes. Like a Roman Empress. Or Audrey Hepburn. Rachel -- or Rache -- as we called her, epitomized beauty and health to woeful ugly duckling me.

Studying her from afar, I couldn't understand my emotional pull. Maybe it was due to the intriguing way she waved slender hands and arms as she spoke, the dainty way she ate, the way she laughed: spontaneously. Or the way she played basketball with athletic ease during R&R. Maybe it was the joy of life she shared with her peers. Her every move thrilled -- and frightened -- because she stirred a deep, forbidden yearning within me. And those violet eyes held me captive.

Finally, I admitted to myself that I had a mammoth crush on her. And it was the first time I felt gloriously alive.

One afternoon, with no planned camp activity, she yelled across the open field where we gathered each morning for Wake-Up call: "JEN.. round up your cabin. I'll get mine! Let's hike!" She couldn't possibly hear my pounding heart.

Walking next to Rache, herding our charges along the trail: *watch out for poison ivy, keep your eyes out for garter snakes…!* I was in heaven. Tongue-tied in heaven.

"What's your high school?" she asked melodically. "What're your plans after graduation? Boyfriend? Family?"

Gradually over the summer, we got to know and trust each other. Only I was careful not to reveal too much. Was so in awe of this raven-haired beauty with the violet eyes I didn't want to say anything that might alienate her. *I'm in love. As simple and as complicated as that. Always on heightened emotions with her. A deep swollen throb in my gut.*

Because I thought it wrong to feel such passion for a girl, I controlled my adoration… until one of the last nights….

Near the end of our camp session, following a raucous Skit Night at the Main Lodge, Rache and I were the only staff members left for clean-up. Later, on the wrap-around wooden verandah facing Silver Lake, we watched a full moon pop out of the black sky from behind clouds. Like a spotlight, splashing its reflection on the still black water. Magic touched us.

"Let's go to the dock."

I nodded, tingling.

On the well-worn grey wooden planks, we sat side by side: four youthful legs dangling in dark lake water. I could smell the sweet golden grass from the field. Inhaled the musty dampness of tall cattails. Heard the deep rumble of bullfrogs on lily pads, a lonely loon call on the lake's belly. My soul drank in the fluorescent moon reflection rippling on the water.

Rache dipped her hand in the lake, flung water drops on my thigh. I shivered deliciously.

More water drops on my skin. I shivered again. Exquisite excitement churned down there.

Then her fingers did the unthinkable. Slowly, deliberately, they walked up my thigh to my crotch. Held my breath. Fire raced through my veins.

"Like that?" she crooned softly, dropping her head on my shoulder.

I purred.

"Guess you do," she whispered into my ear.

Fearfully, hopefully, I turned to face her. Mighty roar of emotions. Her brows arched. Violet eyes searched my blue ones. Closed mine.

We kissed. Gently. Softly. Innocently. Preciously. Then broke. I ached with desire.

Moving closer, she moaned.

"Can't," I barely said.

"Can," she corrected.

We did.

I returned to Roxy's Room a few times, at different hours, over the next weeks. Each time I learned something new from Sweetheart who began welcoming me like an old friend. And she was right about interviewing Raquel who refused to see me.

"Managing a place like this has its pitfalls," Roxy confessed. "Have to change locks a lot for security reasons. Sometimes the girls have accidents on stage, fall in awkward positions. Need a doc. Dancing on the road takes its toll. Easy to get tired, sloppy with your personal safety. Sometimes girls are robbed of their savings if they haven't had time to bank. Sometimes costumes are stolen. Sometimes they get sick. They know they must always look great. Hard when you're not on top of the world. My girls have problems like everyone else. Some have sick kids somewhere. Not an easy business. So when a Raquel doesn't want to talk about her personal self, I'm actually relieved. And not surprised."

Raquel was about to dance for the first time this evening. Deliberately timed my visit to coincide with her performance. Roxy suggested, "Sit up front. Watch her act up close." She studied me for a second. "Know what? You must be about her age! Big difference in lifestyles, eh, lady writer? Compare lifestyles! Now that would make a good story!"

Sat at a table in the second row. A noisy crowd surrounded the stage. Mostly men. A few women, too. MC switched on the mic. Frenzied music thumped, bright lights bounced, all eyes riveted on Raquel winding her way to the front from the back in her skimpy, jungle-patterned bikini. Wanted to study more closely this intriguing woman who unwittingly unlocked a buried memory.

Writhing along her path to the stage, stopping along the way, touching a patron here and there on his cheek, sending him into glorious spasms of lust, she passed me. Paused. Turned. Studied my face. Violet eyes seared into my soul.

As if in a dream, action in the bar wound down to slow motion while rock music banged in the background. Cocking her head, her tangled blonde hair cascading down her back, one piece falling over her forehead, her eyes bored a hole into mine. I couldn't breathe. Feeling that familiar zing.

Approaching, she offered her hand. Her long, red-manicured pointer finger touched my forehead, traced my profile. She looked straight at me. Raised a perfectly shaped eyebrow over a violet eye. Winked.

"Rache?" I whispered absurdly. Leaning forward, frowning. Entranced. Hopeful. Intrigued.

Was that a millisecond flicker of recognition in Raquel's violet eyes?

She blew me a careless kiss, turned away.

Helplessly – longingly -- I watched her tight ass graze the face of an orgasmic guy in front of me as she shimmied her way to the stage.

---3rd place, CAA, Niagara Branch, 2019

Judge's comments: "Someone I Used to Know" begins as a raunchy, sleazy story about a stripper, then lures us into its poignant, lyrical centre, and leaves us with an ending that is so far from being predictable as to be inevitable. But you can only know that when you get there. Among other features the story is remarkable for its vivid depiction of a main character that includes no physical description.

- Colin Brezicki, judge, Fifteen Stories High short story anthology 2019, Canadian Authors Association, Niagara Branch

Stalker

I first saw him from a distance.

At 6:45 a.m. every other day---give or take a few minutes---I ran on the treadmill at KeepFit, glancing out the window in front of me every so often to relieve the boredom of my disciplined run. Each morning I ran on the treadmill he arrived in the parking lot in his shiny black Mazda3 at precisely 7 a.m. Not one minute before. Not one minute after. He always parked in the same spot: third space in from the third row. I noticed him because he was the lone person in the lone car while I was the lone voyeur peering undiscovered out of the tinted gym window that conveniently overlooked the parking lot.

The Mazda guy always followed the same routine.

Engine off, he sat in his car for exactly ten minutes (I checked on the treadmill timer). After ten minutes, he'd open the car door, close it, lock it carefully then test it was locked, walk clockwise around the Mazda slowly, studying it. After three---always three---walks around the car, he strolled towards the mall entrance continually looking back at his car as if it would suddenly sprout wings and fly away. During that ten minutes alone in his car, who knows what he was thinking or doing? He wasn't smoking or talking on a cell phone. Maybe he was listening to the radio. I thought his repetitive behaviour abnormal. Obsessive even.

He was good looking. Average height and build from my vantage point. His face intrigued me and I thought he might be interesting to see at close range. He did have a trim little black beard that looked soft and silky from a distance. Although I couldn't see his eyes, I sensed they were light coloured. Probably blue because he always wore a sky blue jacket, shirt or top.

Idly I began to watch his daily ritual whenever I ran on the treadmill to see if he deviated from it. Each time I watched him, he showed the same compulsive behaviour. It was so weird I even told Glenn, my live-in, about him.

I never knew where this guy was going, where he worked, or if he only stayed in the mall for a short time because after working out two hours, I just wanted to get out of there.

Except this one morning. I was meeting Glenn for grocery shopping later so headed for Tim Horton's in the food court for a quick coffee. That's when I saw him. From the coffee line. The obsessive guy with the trim beard. For a minute he startled me. Even more amazing was how our eyes accidentally met and instantly connected. He had no idea who I was or that I had been spying on him from the second-floor gym window. His penetrating look embarrassed me and I began to wonder if he knew I had been watching him. I sort of smiled half-crookedly and he smiled back. A broad genuine smile.

Suddenly he was beside me.

"Let me buy you coffee," he said.

"But I don't even know you."

"Hi. I'm Bill. Now you know me."

"Thanks," I said, thinking what a cocky so-and-so.

"Join me over at that table." Bill motioned as the cashier gave me my double cream, one sugar java jolt.

And that's how the intro happened. As innocent as you please.

"Name?" he asked with such intensity I paused.

"Pat."

"Hi Pat."

"Hi Bill. So, what am I doing here?" I asked, noticing the dazzling blue colour of his eyes. He wore a flat gold chain around his neck. It settled on a cluster of dark curly hair showing above his solid blue golf shirt that matched his eyes. I had been right about his eyes.

He grinned. "Having coffee with me." He grinned again. Then, staring at my ring finger, he said: "Happily married?"

"Not exactly," I said quickly. "Happily living together."

"Good. Now I know where I stand."

"Hey, Bill…" I stammered. "I don't even…."

"Know me?" he finished.

"Yeah."

"Well, there's not much to know about me. I'm alone drinking my coffee. I see a pretty woman come through the door staring at me and think…why not? Why not enjoy coffee with this pretty woman? That's all."

"Yeah," I smiled and relaxed a little, slightly flattered. Only he didn't know I knew all about his little idiosyncrasies. His daily ritual in his car in the same parking spot. Circling the car three times.

"So," said Bill. "Tell me a little about yourself." Like a babbling fool I did. Told him about Glenn and how we'd been together for five years ("ah," he commented, "my kid sister almost made five years with her live-in…") and that I worked in the local library and loved the outdoor life.

"I can tell that," he interrupted.

"How?"

"You're carrying a gym bag and you just came through the door from KeepFit so I figure someone who stays in such good shape must like the outdoor life." He emphasized *such good shape* saying the words slowly and with deliberation that it slightly unnerved me.

"Anyway," I said. "Gotta go and meet Glenn."

"Your special man."

"Yep."

"Well, nice to meet you, Pat with the golden hair and shining eyes." He looked straight through me and I felt an odd shudder. "What'd you say your last name was?"

"I didn't."

"Well, I'm curious. It's… Smith?"

"What?" I said laughing. "No, it's Ryan."

Then I stopped laughing. Using the oldest trick in the book, he had my last name. I didn't like that because I already knew he was a bit unusual. "Thanks for the coffee, Bill."

"No problem Patricia Ryan."

The way he said my full name bothered me. Damn.

"Bye," I said, "and thanks again." I picked up my gym bag and ran to the parking lot to the car. Something made me look back. I saw Bill watching me get into my white Toyota. Why was this unease slowly spreading over me?

As soon as we connected, I told Glenn what happened and how agitated I felt and for no good reason. Just a strange prickly feeling. "Nonsense," he reassured me. "You librarians read too many books with too many plots and you think a guy whose bought you coffee has some kind of sinister ulterior motive."

That evening the red flag started to wave. About 9 o' clock, the phone rang. Glenn answered. "Who was that?" I asked. "No-one," he said. "A hangup. Probably someone realized they had a wrong number."

Ten minutes later, the phone rang again. "I'll get it this time," I shouted from my downstairs office and hit the button.

"Hello," I said.

"Hi Pat." My heart stopped beating for an instant. I said nothing.

"Have you forgotten me already? It's Bill." I knew damn well who it was and I was annoyed. Still, I knew it was best to downplay my reaction.

"Oh, hi Bill," I said. "Why on earth are you calling?"

"Oh," came the smooth reply. "Just wondering if we could have coffee together again tomorrow, same place, same time."

"No. Sorry," I said in a clipped voice, thinking why am I saying *I'm sorry*?

"No problem," said Bill. "We can always get together another time when it's more convenient for you."

"Sorry, Bill." There I go again with my *sorry* bit, "but it's impossible. You know I'm committed."

"Well, silly me," he taunted. I could feel those penetrating blue eyes piercing me through the phone line. "I didn't ask you to go out with me," he blew softly. "I only asked you for coffee."

"Thanks, but no thanks," I said and quickly hung up. I stared at the phone, breathing hard. What the devil was happening here? Why did I feel so jumpy?

"GLENN!" I yelled running upstairs.

Ten minutes later the phone rang again. "Don't get it!" I shouted. He already answered.

"Another hangup."

"Let's get caller ID," I said, insecurity building in my voice.

On my next workout day, I rushed to the gym at 6:30 a.m. From the treadmill I watched the parking lot like a hawk.

At precisely 7:00 a.m., Bill arrived in his shiny black Mazda. This time I shivered when I saw the car. He parked in the same spot: third space in from the third row. With the engine off, he sat in his car for exactly ten minutes. Then he opened the car door, closed it, locked it, carefully checked the lock, then walked clockwise around the Mazda slowly three times, studying it. Finally, he began to stroll towards the mall entrance all the while looking back at the Mazda.

I ran faster on the treadmill.

Still feeling uneasy after my shower, I decided to ignore Tim Horton's this morning. Grabbing my gym bag, I rushed through the exit.

"Hi."

My heart stopped. It was him. Waiting outside the gym door.

"What are you doing here?" I frowned.

"Hey, Pat, pretty lady with the golden hair and shining eyes," smiled Bill. "Just looking for a little company while I have coffee. You don't have to get so jumpy."

"Look," I said firmly. "I don't really know you. So sorry. No coffee." Damn, there was that 'sorry' again! "Besides, I need to get to work."

"Ah, yes, the library," he smiled. "No problem. We can catch each other another time."

Trembling, I held my breath as I unlocked the Toyota and slid into the driver's seat. When I stole a backwards glance at the mall door, he was standing there. Watching me. I shuddered. Worse, I suddenly spied a note on my windshield under the wipers. Even without opening it, I knew it was from him. When I looked at the mall exit again he was standing there. Waving.

That night I told Glenn about Bill's sudden appearance outside the gym door and showed him the note: *Let's have coffee together Pat.*

"Relax," said easy-going Glenn. But he did frown. "He knows you aren't interested in having coffee. I'm sure you won't see him anymore."

Glenn always sounds so reasonable about everything so I calmed down. That evening, no phone calls.

Each morning I went to the gym now I held my breath. I even considered changing my workout time but then decided no oddball was going to rule my life. Besides, there hadn't been another impromptu meeting with him for a week or so. I slipped into a more relaxed mode.

That is, until one day at work.

I was at my desk when unexpectedly I heard, "Hi there my pretty little Pat with the golden hair and shining eyes."

I didn't have to look up to know it was him. My body stiffened in automatic response.

"What are you doing here?" I said, trying hard to keep my composure while my insides reeled in anger.

"Hey lovely Patsy," he crooned. "Why so upset? This is a public place after all."

His nonchalance and familiarity infuriated me. On top of that, he called me Patsy, a name reserved for Glenn and some close friends. Another emotion crowded my fury, though. Fear. He had obviously and deliberately come looking for me at my place of work. I felt like a bug under a microscope.

"When's your coffee break?" he crooned again, his voice dripping with honey. "I was just chatting with your friend, Nancy, over there. She tells me you're both taking off this weekend for the country with some friends. Gee, sounds like fun. Want another friend to go along too?"

Using all my self-control to remain civil I decided to confront him with what I now considered the Bill problem. "You seem to be following me." I accused. "Are you?"

"Well, Patsy, I don't think so. I may have seen you around over the past days and weeks but you haven't seen me." He grinned. Like the proverbial Cheshire Cat.

"What's that supposed to mean?"

He grinned again. "Well, you and Glenn sure lead an active life. Movies…did you like *Trainwreck*…visiting friends, friends visiting you…looked like nice people, the guy was a little loud… tennis, gardening in the yard.…"

Enraged, I stared at him. "You've been watching us." A shudder caught in my throat.

"No. Just you."

"Please stop!"

"Dear Patsy," he said. "Don't you know I can't? I feel tremendously attracted to you. From the first moment our eyes linked. And I want you to be mine."

"You're crazy." Fear squeezed my heart.

"Only crazy about you."

"Hi there you two!" Nancy breezed by. "Just met Bill a few minutes ago and he told me you guys are friends from way back." And she sailed on by with books in her arms.

With a crooked smile, Bill just looked at me, arching one dark brown eyebrow over a piercing blue eye.

"You're harassing me."

"No-o-o," he said calmly. "We just happen to meet each other once in awhile. That's hardly harassment among friends." He turned to leave. "See ya, Patsy love."

I sat staring after the closed door frozen in my thoughts.

Breathing deeply, I analyzed the situation. Bill was harassing me. I knew there were laws against it. But I couldn't go to the police. I didn't even know his last name. And what he said was true. We didn't see each other but he just rolled off every activity Glenn and I had been doing recently. So, he must be watching us…me. The fear factor raced down my back again.

Our girls' get-together at Nancy's cottage was set for Saturday. I was joining the group later because Glenn and I had business to tend to first. He was leaving his company for another and we were finalizing financial and logistical details. When I finally left for the cottage later in the day, Glenn kissed me on my nose. "Have a great time," he said. I kissed him back. Good, gentle, Glenn. How I had come to appreciate him.

It felt fine to be off by myself. The drive gave me a chance to sort out disturbing thoughts about the Bill dilemma. Glenn was not so complacent about Bill now and insisted I document each time he contacted me and my reaction. If we went to the police, I needed facts. My biggest problem: no personal information on the guy.

Halfway to the lake I casually glanced in the rearview mirror. The traffic had thinned; there was only one car in the distance behind me. I kept an eye on it as the driver slowly inched closer.

Turning left onto the gravel road I checked my rearview mirror again. The car behind me turned left, too. I frowned and a vague uneasiness settled in the pit of my stomach. Then I shook myself: *C'mon Pat. The driver is probably going to a cottage along the road, too.* Truly, I was over dramatizing events.

A gang---or is it a gaggle?---of mature girlfriends guarantees a fun time. We drank early, barbequed late, skinny dipped in the lake, and gossiped. The best kind of freedom day.

I was still recovering from our Saturday party on Monday morning. The ringing phone on my desk was an irritating interruption during the usually early quiet hours in the library. Sighing, I lifted the receiver.

"Hello," his voice purred.

I stiffened.

"Don't hang up," he crooned. "I have something to tell you."

I should have hung up but instead I clung to the receiver, paralyzed. Like a deer at night caught in the headlights of an oncoming car. I realized later I should have picked up a pencil to start recording his words but his call shocked me.

"You have a beautiful body," he breathed. "I was captivated when I saw you in the lake. No clothes on. You're in better shape than any of your friends. I keep looking at the shot I took."

I slammed down the receiver, quivering. Nancy looked over, raised her eyebrows quizzically, then continued cataloguing.

So, the car behind me had been him after all. I should have trusted my gut instinct. But where could he have seen us? Was he on the ridge that ran behind the cottage and beach?

Jittery, I changed my workout time to match Glenn's after his work day. When we met, I told him about the phone call. "Jeez, this is getting serious, Patsy. We've got to lodge a complaint. He's stalking you."

His reaction didn't help. Glenn, always so calm and reassuring, was expressing concern.

"Patsy," he said. "You know I have an overnight in Ottawa this week and now I'm worried about leaving you alone. Why don't you come with me?"

"This is ridiculous, Glenn. We're letting some creep dictate our life. It's crazy. You go ahead. If I really feel nervous, I'll stay with Nance."

When Glenn left for the airport, I was a Nervous Nellie. Reassuringly, he called me constantly. I told him, half-joking but dead serious, that I hid a kitchen knife under the runner on the table by the front door. "Just in case...." I sort of laughed. I didn't tell him I intended to put one under my pillow, too. A long pause on his end.

"Patsy," he breathed. "We have to take decisive action about this stalker creep when I get back. We'll go to the police. I can hardly wait to see you, hold you. Love you, girl."

"Love you, too, big boy," I crooned with much more bravado than I felt.

A pink striated sunset washed the twilight sky the night I was alone. The heat of the day melted with a welcoming evening breeze as I stepped outside to drink in the natural beauty.

Suddenly my peripheral vision caught a fast movement to my right. Quickly turning, I spotted the black squirrel as it rustled among the leaves in the birch tree. He chattered at me as if to say, *you are such a silly goose*! I laughed and took a deep breath.

Chiding myself for overreacting, I gazed down our stone-lined path. That's when I saw him.

With racing heart, I watched Bill casually saunter towards me as if he lived here. When he stood face to face with me on the porch, he stopped. Puzzled, with rising panic, I digested everything that followed in slow motion.

"Good evening, Patsy-Love." His piercing blue eyes terrified me as he inched closer. Casually, he leaned against the porch column. "You must be wondering who I really am...."

Unnerved, I could not answer. Only stared at him.

"Once upon a time," he began slowly as I desperately tried to think of escape... "your loving Glenn broke my little sister's heart. I loved my kid sister with all my heart. Your Glenn led her on a merry chase of pretend love then abandoned her for YOU." I feared how he shook with rage. With narrowed eyes he whispered menacingly, "she was fragile to begin with but after Glenn left she was devastated...."

He paused, shaking, breathing hard, like some monster.

I took a deep breath.

"I vowed I'd hurt your GLENN...." he spit out his name with a shout, "....like he hurt my sister. She killed herself over that worthless piece of shit..." Suddenly, he lunged towards me.

Gasping, horrified, speechless, I reeled away quickly.

With brute force, he pushed me hard and backwards against the door and into the house. The last thing I remembered was reaching for the butcher knife....

- 2015 -1st prize – John Kenneth Galbraith Award

The Pocket Locket

Your legs are long and shapely. And you have a killer smile.

No-one, especially a man, had ever said that to Lucinda. At seventeen, all she ever thought of herself were these awful freckles spread over her face and across her back. Oh, and don't forget her arms. She always wore long sleeves.

And yet, this guy seemed to have noticed her best attributes. Now, if she could only manage to get her hands on a pair of real nylon stockings! She wasn't into phony seam lines women penciled up the back of their legs during these wartime days. He would see through that charade in a minute. He was a guy with talent. An artist.

She whirled happily around the kitchen -- too close to the woodstove -- her blonde hair carefully styled in Victory Rolls.

"Lucy!" warned her mom. "Get away from the stove! You polish the silver yet? You know company's comin' for dinner."

Lucy's mother. A saint when she wanted to be. A witch when she didn't get her way. She was prone to fake fainting spells that once terrified Lucy and her sister, Blanche, both thinking mom had something terribly wrong with her. Years later their family doctor explained those fainting spells were fake, a cry for attention. But Lucy and Blanche didn't know it then.

The year was 1941, and despite war measures and sanctions, Lucy was floating on air.

Gregory, her artist admirer -- a romantic and adventurer -- attracted her with his sky-blue eyes and thick, dark, wavy hair, one errant lock tumbling over his forehead. Swimming laps in Doe Lake developed his upper body strength, he said, when she admired his toned muscles.

"Don'tcha dare get with fam'ly, Lucy!" warned mom. "I won't have another one of you girls bringin' shame on this house." She minced no words about Blanche, her wayward daughter. Then it was back to Greg. "And why isn't he in uniform? Anyone worth anythin' would've signed up by now."

It was hard to ignore her mother's rantings. It was true. Blanche, at 18, was already an unmarried mom. Her chubby baby girl was curly-headed and well-loved but Blanche -- and Lucinda -- knew she faced a hard life without a father. Plus, a hill of scornful gossip heaped on the young unwed mother. *She's a bad girl, loose girl, cheap hussy, embarrassin' her family. And her father workin' hard at the factory to put food on the table. Turrible, they said.*

Meanwhile, Greg, a shy, possessive guy, had his own quirks. He didn't want to share Lucy with anyone. Locking fingers, the couple wandered alone along meandering country roads. Together, they watched, fascinated, at the nearby river while a beaver, its nose above the surface, pushed fallen branches to its mud-packed dome home. They caught a brown-eyed doe peering tentatively at them through the leaves of trees. Marvelled at monarch butterflies flitting through wildflower-studded fields. And, despite her mom's dire warnings, Lucy made passionate love with her guy on a gray wool blanket that made Lucy's skin itch.

In the afterglow of after-love, with the sun still strong in the sky, Greg offered Lucy a cigarette. He rolled his own between nicotine-stained fingers. "No, thank you," she said at first.

"Let me light one for you," he said. Lit it between his lips, took it out, handed it to her. Just like in the movies. She could smell him on that cigarette. They smoked together, she inhaling superficially, sitting against the trunk of a wild apple tree as the sun sank low on the horizon. She ached in the pit of her stomach: a heavenly, gut-wrenching delicious pull in her groin. She adored this man.

"Signed up. Finally," he said nonchalantly. As if talking about signing one of his paintings.

Her heart fluttered. She half-hummed, half-sang the hit tune *Boogie Woogie Bugle Boy* by the Andrews Sisters in celebration. She didn't want to betray her real feelings of fear.

He smiled, wrapped his arm around her freckled shoulders, drew her in. "Like my dad. A hero in the last war. Family expects this. Specially since Mom was a British war bride. Dad brought her here after the war ended. She wanted to go back to England when she saw how poor he was. But," he said, "she's now the mother of eight."

Lucy knew Greg had spent a year with his mother's wealthier family in Sussex, England. He loved the experience and didn't want to return to Canada.

"But what about your art scholarship? What about your future?" She wanted to say 'our' future but was too afraid.

"No matter what, we'll be together, Luce," he said matter-of-factly, reading her mind. Cigarette smoke curled lazily towards the blue sky. "You're mine." So definitive. She tingled.

She looked at him sideways. Loved his straight, aristocratic nose, his strong profile, his take-charge manner.

"We'll marry soon's we can." Didn't ask her. Took it for granted. She trembled within. Thrilled by his possessiveness.

He got up, casually flicked his cigarette into the lake. Took hers, did the same. Pushed her gently back down on that itchy blanket and took her again. She had no doubt this man was hers. And she was his. Body and soul intertwined.

One day he came calling for her in his air force uniform. Her mother's eyes shone with admiration at his sight.

Lucinda swooned all over again. He looked twice as handsome in that uniform.

They -- no, it was Greg -- decided to elope.

He said they would marry in the small church on the hill. "In two days. Tell no-one. Especially your mother." He had talked to the Rev.

Marriages in a hurry were common these days. Too many boys headed overseas. Too many girls left behind. Too many love stories left hanging.

"Wear my favourite hat," he ordered passionately. She knew the one: navy blue with a wide, flat brim adorned with a pale pink velvet ribbon. She liked it, too. Hid her freckled face.

She did not tell her sister Blanche. Nor her mother. Nor her hard-working father. Funny, she thought, the one person she wished could be there was her father. Kind. Gentle. Overworked. Weary. An old soul. And a loving one.

The minister was busy marrying young couples that Saturday in June. The church's austere interior was softened with the sight of many couples: young men -- boys really -- in uniform, girls in their Sunday best, some lucky ones even wore nylon stockings! Carrying bouquets of roses mixed with wildflowers from the hills. Wearing large, floppy wide-brimmed hats that perched seductively over their Victory Rolls.

Lucinda looked down with pride at her Mary Jane ankle strap pumps. Borrowed from her best friend. Her feet might hurt but she looked glamorous. For Greg. *My husband.* She swirled the words around in her mouth and liked the taste. Her heart hammered when she whispered *husband.*

Whatever happened now, they were together. Lucinda was in heaven with her handsome serviceman in his blue grey uniform and the jaunty side cap trying vainly to tame his tousled hair.

Life at their lakeside honeymoon cottage hidden among birch trees was a continuous tumble in bed. He constantly sketched her in the nude. In every position. From every angle. When she saw herself on paper, without her ever present freckles, she shivered with delight. Their heads came up occasionally for a meal or two but they thrived mostly on passion.

Until a shocking visit from the RCAF Special Police.

"Flight Sergeant Air Gunner Greg Brittain?" barked an official voice at the door.

Greg and Lucinda were sunbathing in the nude on the flat cottage roof. Her heart raced. What was wrong?

Greg peered over the roof edge, his bare buttocks touching her bare stomach. "Here."

"You're under arrest for being AWOL," barked the official. "Come with us. Now!"

That was the end of their sinfully romantic honeymoon. Four heavenly days and nights together.

"I'm pregnant," she whispered as they led him away. "I know I am."

"You'd better be," he smiled in return.

When they parted before he sailed overseas, he stroked her wet cheek softly, gently nuzzling her tears into his warm skin. Reverently touched her abdomen. "I'm comin' back, kid. You be sure to wait for me. You and Babe."

Tears flowing, she pressed a silver heart-shaped locket inscribed with L that held her photo inside, into his hand. "Keep it with you always for good luck," she sobbed. "I'll write every day." And she did.

Their pregnancy was confirmed after he left. She wrote him the exciting news. Said she was very sick. Her family doctor smiled with compassion: "I understand you're worried. Go home. Get a cup of coffee. Light a cigarette. Put up your feet and relax." She followed his advice while listening to Vera Lynn's *We'll Meet Again* on the radio. And she wept with fear over their unknown future together.

***

In her family's fields in the late afternoon, Lisbeth De Vries watched the parachute descend from the overcast sky. Once a thriving farm, the land had been decimated by Nazi troops who had invaded The Netherlands in 1940. Now, almost two years later, with the early arrival of Spring, green shrubs and leafy trees shielded the ugly from sight.

During the Occupation, Lisbeth had changed from a fun-loving teen to a nervous, frightened young woman, aware of her family's precarious position in an enemy-infested country.

Through her *vader*'s bargaining, she had been spared the unthinkable: taken away to tend to the sexual needs of enemy soldiers. Instead, she and her father were forced to play host in their farm home to a German *commandante* who liked Lisbeth's soft limbs and the fresh food of the land.

Her father had visibly aged knowing his only child lay nightly in her parents' double bed at the mercy of a Nazi officer. Before papa died -- from heartache she was certain -- he cried quietly in Lisbeth's arms trying to explain his rationale: if she insisted on staying during the war, he wanted her to eat well and live in her own home during this dreadful hell. No other man would dare touch the *commandante's* mistress.

Her *moeder*, Wilhelmina, would have negated this horrific arrangement with all her strength. But she did not know. She had left for her sister's home in Canada before the Occupation. And she had wanted her only child with her.

But Lisbeth had fought to remain with her father and refused to leave.

The stubborn Dutch trait, he had accused her. "Maybe it will save you in the end," he said.

Lisbeth had watched other parachutists descend from the dangerous skies over Apeldoorn, only to be seized by Nazis as they landed. The parachute her eyes now followed from behind the barn had appeared after a blinding aerial explosion. She assumed enemy gunfire had ripped into the Allied aircraft.

She watched the chute pop open and a lone figure dangle from the end of its nylon cord. The parachute swayed in the wind. As it hit the ground, she heard the violent thud not far from her hiding spot. Lisbeth waited for Nazi soldiers to descend as always, like a pack of snarling hyenas. But there was no movement from surrounding fields and land. Still, she waited a little longer.

When darkness began to spread across the sky, Lisbeth ventured forth. Tentatively she walked, then rushed, towards the sprawling parachute. When she knelt, she knew the airman was barely alive. His back was bent in an unnatural position, one leg at an awkward angle to his cord-tangled body. Blood trickled from his nose and one ear. Dead, she thought, thankful it was so swift for the young soldier.

But his blue eyes suddenly opened wide. In pain. She remembered later how bright they were, even in the dark. She touched his cheek. Already it was cold. Bent to kiss it. She didn't want him to die alone. He tried to speak. Hoarsely. Slowly.

"Lucy," he moaned.

"Yes," she whispered into his ear.

She studied his handsome face. Deduced he was her age. She saw the winged RCAF patch on his leather flight jacket. Caught sight of an artist's calligraphy on its front. Read quickly: *Lucy.*

He moaned again. She nestled closer. Smelled his masculinity. Lucy must be his wife? Girlfriend? she wondered.

Reaching into his jacket pockets, she felt around for some ID. Instead, out fell a silver locket inscribed with the letter 'L'. Lisbeth knew it must be special. She rescued it. Held it. Whispered: *I promise to return it to Lucy.* And stroked his forehead.

His lips parted to say something. Then closed again.

Not much later, after he died, she lifted his cold hand to her cheek, pressed it close. Glancing around, she still saw no enemy. Ran for the safety of the farmhouse. Soon enough they would find him.

In the kitchen, she sobbed. For her father. Her mother. Herself. Her own ruined body. For the dead airman in the field. She knew she would remember his last word: *Lucy.* Someday, somewhere, it might make sense. Her fingers played idly with the locket's silver chain. Curious, she opened the heart and studied the pale photo of a young woman.

Forlorn, she looked around the warm and comfortable room once stocked with fresh, bountiful produce. Empty now except for tulip bulbs, their remaining sustenance. Even the *commandante* was short on bringing back supplies from town headquarters. Troops were restless. She sensed an aura of change.

***

After the war, when Lisbeth was reunited with her mother in Ontario, she recognized how far apart they had grown. She never shared details of her father's heartbreaking death. Nor the stillborn birth of her baby -- the *commandante*'s son -- whom she could never grieve. Her life in Canada provided a new beginning.

Her hospital job near Trenton brought her into contact with many young shell-shocked soldiers: maimed, broken in spirit. Not one woman or man returned the same person as when they had left.

She met and married Ted while he was recuperating from his Overseas service. They rented a townhouse -- in a complex of many -- on the outskirts of the city. During the summer, neighbours -- all women -- gathered on the combined front lawns to enjoy one other. Children ran around and between their mothers' lawn chairs. Laughter filled the air.

"Lucy!" yelled a seated woman to a latecomer. "Over here!" she beckoned.

Lisbeth stopped digging up tulip bulbs from around her front steps when she heard the name. Looked idly over at the circle of women. 'Lucy' was approaching the group with a lawn chair on one arm while holding a little girl's hand with her other.

Lisbeth studied the young mother. She looked to be about the age of the dying airman.

Lisbeth's heart began to beat a little faster. She looked over at the circle of young women. Watched this Lucy. Felt an immediate compelling connection. She retreated to the back of her mind and sank onto the cement patio edge in front of her unit. It was probably a coincidence, of course, but the name tugged at the jagged edges of her memory: the downed airman in her field uttering *Lucy* with his dying breath. The silver locket inscribed with L inside his flight jacket. Inside the heart, a young woman's photo.

She looked over again at the young mother. Studied her again. And the little girl by her side.

At the same time, horrific flashbacks seized her. The naked, hairy *commandante* holding her down in bed. Thrusting. Night after night. She, wretching. Blood. Blue baby. The smell of Death.

It was all there, in vivid colour, as if the war had happened yesterday.

Laying down the trowel, Lisbeth slowly turned, entered her townhouse, walked upstairs to their bedroom where she kept her jewelry box.

Her fingers scrounged among loose beads, detached bracelets, tangled costume adornments, out-of-date brooches. All lying in a messy heap on the bottom drawer of her jewelry box. Fingers searched for, and touched, the forgotten locket.

Slowly lifting the silver chain with the L inscribed locket from the junky accessories, she stared at the silver heart. Picked it up delicately. Walked to the bedroom window from where Lisbeth could watch – again -- the women in a semi-circle of lawn chairs embracing the late-comer Lucy.

Opened the locket. Looked at the young mother on the lawn and looked at the locket. Looked again. And again. There seemed to be a resemblance.

Should she venture out to the lawn and approach the young woman because of some sentimental hunch?

Slowly, she circled the room, stared again at the photo, then out the window. Startled, she suddenly heard the car door slam in the driveway, signaling that Ted had arrived home from work.

Lisbeth sighed, crossed the room, returned the locket to her jewelry box.

Tomorrow, she thought, she might approach the young mother, Lucy, and her daughter.

-- lst Honourable Mention, 2023 Royal Canadian Legion Ontario Command, District E Seniors Literary Competition (short story category)

Twelve Wild Women and One Outhouse

Before tattoos, body jewellery and thongs were common, we were twelve young women who bonded while attending Ottawa's oldest and most historical high school, part of the "Class of 1960".

Our group included a head girl, basketball player, cheerleaders, Girls' AA leaders, Hi-Y members and high school yearbook staffers. How could we know then that we twelve young women would fan out in different directions of the world and yet maintain our bond, albeit sporadically, over more than 60 years? And who would guess these same twelve women -- at sixty-five years old -- would get together again to celebrate their sisterhood?

Cottage country reunion

That's exactly what happened with the "Longlasters" reunion over four sun-filled summer days at a McGregor Lake cottage in Québec in 2007. One common discovery: although our divergent life experiences had shaped our growth and development throughout adulthood, our core values and close friendship ties remained intact.

After university, which we all attended and which was a new phenomenon in our era, two of us joined CUSO (Canadian University Services Overseas) landing in India and Ghana respectively. Those two-year commitments led to a successful professional East Indian Classical Dance career for one and the launching of scholarships for female students in Ghana by the other.

One of us taught in the Canadian North and Newfoundland. Another founded an alternative approach to education in Toronto. A third taught Tai Chi for over 20 years. Another was an economist working in Ireland.

Transitional Age

As one of our group puts it: "we represented the transitional age" for women. Our models at the time were stay-at-home moms; the academic environment then did not encourage us in careers. We had to learn what we had not been taught. So, we worked outside the home and raised children simultaneously, some of us at careers that were male-dominated at the time. We each found success in our fields; in fact, we represented examples of "firsts."

One was a film guru who received a Visionary Leadership Award from the Canadian film industry as well as the Queen's Silver Jubilee Medal awarded to young Canadian achievers under 40.

Also among us were professional writers, editors and a publisher, an economist, a nurse, a chartered accountant, school teachers, and a leading advocate for establishment of a National Botanical Garden in Ottawa.

Only one outhouse

McGregor Lake was the perfect catalyst for our reunion. Unfortunately, we had access to only one outhouse. Fortunately, the one-holer was tastefully decorated with ceramic cherubs. Still, it wasn't a fluid change from indoor plumbing. Those mosquitoes! Bugs! Creepy crawly creatures! That awful smell!

And being women with weak bladders from childbirth, stumbling our way in the middle of the night to the unlit outhouse in the darkness of a country sky, guided only by a flashlight beam, was fraught with danger from unseen creatures and obstacles.

Swimming au naturel

Foregoing daily routines back home, inhibitions due to flabby stomachs and fleshier bodies disappeared: We swam and played in the nude as we leapt eagerly back to nature. We listened to the plaintive call of the loon, remembered former crushes, camping days and campfires together. We devoured a calorie-rich birthday cake after an enthusiastic chorus of "Happy Birthday to us!"

In the wee hours of morning, we serenaded the lake's cottagers with loud songs, sung off-key and accompanied by bawdy jokes and copious bottles of wine. We shared stories and hopes and fears and philosophies and health hints. Our only injuries: A foot splinter from the dock and a nasty insect bite.

Our new roots

We gathered from Ireland and across Canada: Halifax, Edmonton, Salt Spring Island, Burlington, Peterborough Toronto, Rigaud and Ottawa. Together we've raised 23 children, adore our many grandchildren, and seven of us remain married to our first husbands (statistically unusual?)!

One of our group members, a well-known Ottawa landscape artist who suffered a degenerative disease, was unable to join us. So, we did the next best thing. As a city art gallery was showcasing her work, we left cottage country to view her canvases created with her love of nature. Then -- her preference -- we spent an evening chatting with her by phone.

On our last day together--as we prepared to scatter back to our respective homes--we received a surprise visitor. A male classmate, who heard our raucous singing across the lake, turned up to add to our glory stories.

High School Sketches

With a touch of nostalgia, I glance today at a few of the personality sketches in our 1960 high school graduating yearbook. Idealistic, innocent, they are a testimony to our youthful optimism. *"Go West, young girl, go West"; "Laughter is the spice of life"; "She's just what she is, what better report: A girl, a friend, and a good sport"; "Everything succeeds with people of cheerful disposition"; "Laugh and the world laughs with you"; "Sweet personality, full of rascality..."*

Fast Forward

Eleven not-so-wild women reunited on Canada's west coast four years ago. Over the years it seems getting together has become more difficult. A challenge.

Along the way to 2023, we lost one of us. In 2018, our Classical Indian dancer died after losing her battle to myeloma. Her death brought home the realization that we are mortal.

Death also took the lives of some of our loved ones.

And a few of us have battled – successfully -- serious diseases, like cancer.

Now what?

Our wild group of 12 is now 11. This year we celebrate our 80th birthdays. We talk about another reunion but I think it unlikely. Some of us don't like to travel anymore. Some can't. We keep in touch via emails and social media.

Ignorant

In recent years, we have come to recognize our guilty sins. We (unknowingly and unwittingly) were cavalier in our environmental treatment of this precious earth. Weren't the fish going to live forever in the sea? Those pristine Ontario lakes where we camped. Wouldn't they always remain the same?

And those inexcusable Residential Schools. Why were we never aware of them? Why were we never aware of the tragic plight of our Indigenous brethren?

The Last Call

Once wild women, we tread more softly now, each of us soberly aware we must face the realities of aging and our inevitable end.

In the innocence of our youth and the twilight of our years, we recall a less complicated life in Canada. Our country has changed. We have changed.

And I know we could never tolerate an outhouse now.

- Published in Story Quilt, 2023

The Road To Hell

Satisfied and smug, we stuffed the final pieces of straw into our life-size, life-like mannequin.   Hallowe'en was the perfect time to test the reality of our creation. Standing up our version of Frankenstein in front of a makeshift brace, we four rang the stranger's doorbell. Then quickly hid behind juniper bushes shielding us from view.

The door opened and the quintessential little old lady stepped forth holding a dish filled with candy. As she held out her goodies, our strawman collapsed and fell in a heap on the porch.

The old lady screamed. We collapsed in giggling hysteria as she slammed shut her door.

On a high now, we continued from house to house pulling the stunt over and over. After witnessing our scheme's wild success --- and growing bored with its predictable response --- we decided to up the ante.

A great idea hit us collectively. The highway overpass presented the perfect opportunity. We'd throw our straw man over the bridge onto the road below just as a car came careening into sight.

And that's exactly what we did.

The driver of the car slammed on his brakes as our mannequin hit the road in front of him. With squealing tires, he pulled over to the side while we ran to hide in the nearest cover. Heard him curse and swear and then start up the hill with a flashlight.

We scattered, of course. Except me.

Reasoning our victimized driver would think no-one would hide near her crime scene, I hid in a nest of evergreens, just off the overpass. Meanwhile, my friends were running like the wind across it.

Big mistake.

Glued to my spot, I watched the beam from his flashlight jump around the conifers. My heart stopped. Thrashing through the trees, he methodically swept the beam back and forth. Back and forth.

The beam stopped. Oh, too close.

Dropping my head facedown onto a floor of dried pine needles, I lay prostrate on the cold earth. Barely breathing. Waiting for the beam --- and him --- to pass.

Suddenly I felt a rough punch on my back. Strong fingers clutched the collar of my coat. Fear set in as he hauls me to my feet. Can't see his face. But I do see the Canada toque he is wearing. His angry eyes flash like red lights.

"Think that's funny, do you?" he shouts. His spit hits my face.

I shake.

"Realize you could have caused a god-damn accident!?" he shouts.

I tremble.

"You're comin' with me, Blondie!" Twists my arm behind my back. Pushes, punches me down the slope to his car pulled over to the side.

"Get in!" A command. I feel his fury. He slams shut the back door. Jumps into the front. Locks the doors.

Am whimpering now. "Sorry. I'm so sorry."

"Just shut the fuck up you little priss."

A nightmare, I tell myself. But I'm not waking up. Quivering in the back of his moving car. Suddenly nauseated.

"Gonna be sick! Pull over! Please!"

"You think I'm falling for that little trick! If you're sick, you damn well gonna clean it up Blondie!"

He's driving like a madman. Speeding. Am so scared. Wetting myself. Can't talk. Weeping. Wailing. What the hell will happen?

Suddenly he curses. I glance out the front windshield. Loose dog tears across the road. In front of us. He swears non-stop. Swerves. Tires squeal. Hit a curb. He loses control. Car skids on its side now. Crunches.

For a second, total darkness. The man is kind of hanging mid-air inside the car. His safety belt held. No sound. No air bag inflation.

I'm thrown against the far door. No safety belt. Curl up in a fetal position.

Hold my breath.

I listen. No sound from the front seat. No breathing. See only the back of the man's head. Hanging to one side. Still wearing his toque.

For an eternity, I sit, silent, my body pushed against the door against the ground.

Thinking. How to escape?

Hear sirens. Squealing stop of a police car.

Flashlight shines into the car. This time I welcome the beam.

Police see me. In a caring voice, they tell me to stay still. Remain calm. They will get me out.

"The driver?" I ask. Afraid to know.

"Think he's in serious condition, miss. Unconscious. Ambulance on its way."

"You know this man?" asks one officer.

"No." Am telling the truth. "He forced me into this car."

I hear conversation.

"Don't panic. We'll get you out, miss."

They do. Very carefully.

Then, "you need to be checked out in the hospital."

"Who is he?" they ask again after they make sure I'm okay.

"I don't know. He forced me into his car. I was terrified." My face starts to screw up as if I'm about to cry.

An officer holds me.

Red lights flash. Ambulance arrives.

Attendants work to remove the man with the toque from his hanging harness.

I watch. Terrified. Transfixed.

As they release the man's body, his toque falls off.

Don't bat an eyelash when I see them. Two horns. They are slightly curved. One on either side of his forehead.

That's when I knew I had been on the road to Hell.

--Pick of the Day, CommuterLit 2020

MamaMantra

opleasedeargodhelpme.helpmeplease.Icannotkeeplivin glikethis.osweetjesushelpmegetthroughthissomeonepleaselisten helpme...

Jims--or was it Mims?--was crying. Again. Not a whimper. Or a short sob. A full-fledged wail.

Mama had just closed her eyes, hadn't she? Squinting in the dark at the digital clock radio on their bedside table, she frowned. Luminous dials glowed 4:00 a.m. Beside her, dead to the world like a sleeping babe (ha!), lay Dave. How could he sleep through the twins' razor cut screams?

Mama shut her eyes. Maybe the wailing would cease.

No. Louder now. Better pick-up Mims--she was sure it was her from the shrillness-- sounded female--before she woke up her brother.

Mama rolled out of the sleepy warmth of bed. Brain fog rolled in.

PleasedearGoddon'tletherwakeupherbrother.notsureihaveenou ghstrengthforthembothrightnow.

She felt the tender fullness of her breasts. Her nipples leaking. Mama was such a petite woman it surprised everyone when she said she was breastfeeding both babies.

Stumbling down the hall, she slipped into Mims' bedroom. Yes, she'd been right. It was their girl. Quickly she picked up the open-mouthed sobbing babe and cooed. "S'alright, Mims, mama's here...mama's right here." Swaddling the babe, she settled into the padded Amish rocking chair. She soothed and fussed and guided Mims' searching mouth to her flowing breast. At least this time she only had one suckling babe. Easier on her arms. And her body!

Quiet now except for the snorting, satisfying sucking sounds from Mims.

While rocking and feeding Mims, Mama strained her ears. Listening for some sound, hopefully none, from her sleeping brother, Jims. So far, nothing. He must be immune to his sister's screams, she decided. These clever little people probably figured all this out together in her womb.

In this dark room, with one suckling child at her breast and silence at last, Mama reflected on her life since the birth of their fraternal twins a few months ago. What life? As far as she was concerned, she was a cow, a milk machine that could not satiate her babies. All signs pointed to babies' weight gain and doctor's approval, so she must be producing enough milk.

For no reason, Mama started sobbing. Weeping. *omygodhelpmeamIgoingtomakeit?*

With Mims nursing quietly at her breast, Mama casually examined her own body through wet eyes. Her broken, torn body. The caesarean birth cut had not yet healed so she could see the angry scar snaking across her belly skin. Those ugly varicose veins that seemed to bulge overnight in her aching right leg during her pregnancy were still there and still blue-coloured. Her hormones continued to play havoc with her mental health which left her sometimes out of control, causing her overflow sob sessions. Overwrought. Her raw emotions sat at the edge of an imaginary cliff. Fatigue? She never knew fatigue until she had to care for two babies at once. Her eyelids drooped. She kept looking for a place to lie down, close her eyes, and sleep forever.

A few weeks ago, a couple of nosy co-workers had dropped by with gifts to see her and Mims and Jimmy. They ooh-ed and aww-ed over the babes who loved the attention and gurgled and farted tiny sounds and smiled and cooed.

But her colleagues' casual remarks about Mama's appearance stung her fragile ego, left her wallowing in self-pity after they tripped gaily back to work.

"You do look tired, mama, but still great. Of course. The office guys want to know if you still have your shapely ass. We'll have to report that luscious cleavage. Won't say a word that you're still in Limbo Land. Ruins their image of your perfect body. (At this point, mama self-consciously touched her ratty long, dark locks, unwashed for days.) Well, one of the babes is crying so we better let you get back to it…but we're rootin' for you, mama!"

She wished she'd slammed the door at their retreat but was afraid she'd awaken Jims. He was always the sleepy babe. Mims was always the little hussy.

This early morning Mama rocked while Mimsy sucked on her nipple. The babe's eyes had closed. *Oh no*, thought Mama, *don't sleep now, Mimsy, cuz you haven't had enough. I don't need you to wake up when I'm feeding Jimsy.*

No use. Mimsy's head lolled backwards, eyes closed, mouth open but not sucking. Worse, Mama could smell her dirty diaper. She'd have to wake the baby to change her and then what would follow? Would she drink more then with a clean bottom? Would Jimsy wake up and want his share immediately?

Omygawd,helpme.Ineedtokeepgoing.howmanymonthsaretheynow?CanIstartthemonsolidfood?

As she carefully settled Mims on her side in her crib with the bumper pad of flower and honeybee decals protecting her from the cool green wall, she heard Jimsy stir. In a moment, she knew, he will begin his plaintive cry.

Dave came in then while holding his cup of java. "Gotta run, babe. Looks like everything's under control. They'll soon be old enough to walk and things'll get better. You'll see!" He kissed the air around her.

She heard the garage door open, then close. And he was off before she could blink her tired eyes. Off to a real world with real people who talked real words, ate real food, and asked him how were the twins? How's their Mama? And Dave would reply, oh, everyone's fine, thanks. Mama's a little tired but everything's jist fine.

He never added, she hoped, that she didn't look like the gorgeous babe he'd married. Giving birth to twins takes its toll, y' know, he'd say. Sex? You kidding? Wouldn't want to touch their Madonna.

Mama picked up her crying Jims and, sitting once again in the Amish rocking chair, began the same feeding ritual. Opposite breast.

Settling into her arms, his mouth found her nipple which he snatched in his gummy mouth and sucked thirstily, sometimes a sweet sensation, sometimes painful. His tiny fingers wound around her little finger as Mama murmured again,

ogodhelpmethroughthisIneedYourhelp.don'tletmelosemymind.Helpmeplease.

After feeding and changing his piss-soaked onesie, she lay Jimsy down on his stomach in his crib surrounded by a wallpaper of colourful cowboys and crazy creatures and watched him wriggle his way into the padded corner. Thumb in his mouth. Eyes closed. Content.

Mama tiptoed down the hall to the messy kitchen. No time to clean up anymore. Her exhausted mind registered empty cartons of fast food stacked in the corner of the crowded counter. What was a half-eaten cheese sandwich doing here? She needed to get a wash in, too. The twins were running out of clothes.

Quickly, before the one thousandth interruption, she poached an egg, plunked it on dry brown toast while cocking her head, ever listening for a stir, a cry, a movement from either babe. Dave had left some lukewarm coffee. She reheated it, sat there, her blank mind in a catatonic state.

Clicked on the laptop lying on the side counter. Hit Spotify. Looked at the Playlist. Enya. She was in the mood for Enya: haunting, soothing, calling her name. Peace.

Actually finished her modest breakfast without interruption--always listening for a cry, murmur, stirring--with no noise she began to worry. About the state of their health. Hurrying to their rooms, she muttered:

ogodpleasedon'tletanythinghappentothempleaselookafterthemi'msorryi'vecomplained...

She leaned over Mimsy's crib. This cherub with the insane crop of black hair still lay peacefully on her side. Mama could see/feel her even breathing, watched her tiny chest move up and down, up and down. She was all right.

She hustled to Jimsy's side. He was on his back, tiny hands curled into tiny fists, long eyelashes feathering his closed eyes. She reached down, gently touched his chest. Needed reassurance he was still breathing. Up and down. In and out. Yes, Jimsy was breathing, too.

In a moment of bewilderment, she burst into tears. These two perfect little creatures were entirely in her care. She could never again watch a cat or dog mama protecting their wriggling litters with pride--not realizing their babies would soon disappear from mama's warmth and sloppy kisses to waiting pet owners--without feeling these same overwhelming emotions of helplessness, hopelessness, fear, and overpowering love.

Immediately, she thought of other moms and babes caught in war-torn conflicts around the world, and mourned openly for them. How could they ever cope? Survive? A mother's love is painfully raw.

A plaintive moan escaped her bowed head. Again, she mumbled her Mamamantra...

ogodpleasedon'tletanythinghappentothempleaselookafterthemi'msorryi'vecomplained...

Fun Fact re 'Yesterday' story on next page:

*** A trick called "gunwale bobbing" or "gunwaling" allows a canoe to be propelled without a paddle. The canoeist stands on the gunwales, near the bow or the stern, and squats up and down to make the canoe rock backward and forward. This propulsion method is inefficient and unstable; additionally, standing on the gunwales can be dangerous. However, this can be turned into a game where two people stand one on each end, and attempt to cause the other to lose balance and fall into the water, while remaining standing themselves.*

Yesterday

I close my eyes.

Immediately, I am at camp again. On the banks of the Ottawa River on a wooded, 40- hectare haven. Living with five other girls my age --- early teens --- in a bell tent. Girl Guide members, we bonded during the school year. Now we live together for a few weeks each summer at Camp Woolsey. Away from parents, home, and responsibilities. Pure bliss.

This particular year, in a lucky twist of fate, we five have landed positions on Woolsey's waterfront staff. Our jobs bring prestige, privilege. Meaning we don't have to peel mountains of potatoes or wash dishes in the Mess Hall. Such duties are relegated to mere campers.

Lessons in life

However, no matter inclement weather or cold grey river water or black flies, our job is to teach swimming, canoeing, and water safety to campers. All day. Every day.

Gunwale bobbing** on canoes was our popular time-off pastime. Today, this game played astride gunwales/sides of a canoe, is outlawed. Too dangerous. Liability insurance is now necessary. And yet, gunwale bobbing gave us the opportunity to take chances, to learn how to balance, to fall into the water and get up again. Valuable life lessons.

Night adventure

In the evening, after campfire songs like Land of the Silver Birch, Fire's Burning, and Taps, we were expected to tumble into our tents and sleeping bags, and sleep. Except we waterfront girls never followed protocol. After leaders finished their 'bedcheck', we crept out of our tent and raced onto the path behind our site. Circulating rumours of a boys' camp not far away had piqued our interest. We decided to raid it.

Unfortunately, traipsing along a woodland path in the dark proved difficult. Especially when unidentifiable bush noises alerted suspicious leaders that not all was normal. Also, our *no flashlight* rule to avoid detection was a liability. Despite our precautions, our deviously responsible leaders came looking. We dove into nearby shrubbery to escape discovery. When we thought it safe --- once they paraded past our hiding spot --- we ran for cover back into our tent. All this in darkness.

The next morning, we awoke with terrible rashes covering our bodies. Rashes that itched and oozed with sores. Seems, in our haste to hide, we hid in a patch of poison ivy. (To this day, I swear we saw smirks on our leaders' faces.)

Retaliation

Of course, we must retaliate. Anonymously. We hope. There were no modern bathroom facilities at camp. But there were those old-fashioned outhouses (with carved half-moons in the door of a small wooden latrine) set apart, due to unsavoury odours, from the campsite. One was designated for campers. The other outhouse, farther away and delicately surrounded by greenery, belonged to camp leaders. Cleaning these latrines and throwing lye crystals on the odious contents plopped below the hole was tantamount to hell. While some kept vigilant watch, the rest of us took on the smelly job of exacting our revenge. We opened the leaders' latrine door, lifted the toilet seat, secured plastic wrap across the 'hole', replaced the toilet seat, left the little wooden building and hid in the surrounding shrubbery, ignoring the swarms of eternal buzzing insects.

Didn't take long before a leader needed to answer the call of nature. She ambled along the path to the executive latrine. Stifling giggles, we watched her step inside. Lock the door. We heard her screams. Immediately fled the scene. Tried hard to silence loud snickers.

Yesterday

But all this innocent tomfoolery was yesterday. Now I must return to today and the current sad state of our besieged world. Besides, it's almost time for dinner. What can I possibly prepare that isn't too expensive and that all three kids and their father will eat?   *- published in Daytripping, Summer 2023*

You Can't Go Back

You can't go back, murmur the pundits. You can learn from the past but you can't go back.

One of my sisters and I don't follow rules very well. We did go back. To our childhood home in SmallTown, Ontario. Where gossip and wild spaces and fresh garden vegetables and yes, even sexual innuendos, educated us city slickers in a way no other place could.

Chimney Fire

Like, I still hear the fire sirens in my brain. I was in Grade 5, Marlane in Grade 1. We shared a second-floor bedroom in a heritage brick home on Main Street: complete with a multi-angled ceiling, one small window, and a long no-door closet with steeple-shape interior.

It was 6 a.m. on a freezing morning. My father was up already, stoking coal into the basement furnace, before heading to his job via commuter car to the Big City.

Suddenly he burst into our bedroom where we were still sleeping. "Get up! Get out! Chimney fire! Forget dressing! Just get out!" Then he headed for our brother's bedroom.

That's when I realized the fire sirens were heading to our house! Marlane and Bro shot out of bed. Disappeared down the stairs.

But, me, well, I had rollers in my hair. Good grief, I couldn't go outside with rollers in my hair! What if people saw me like this? I quickly crouched before the mirror whipping out curling rollers, styling my hair into a more presentable shape.

"Good GAWD!" yelled my father as he tore back into the bedroom. (Fire engines stopped outside now. Sirens still howling. Firefighters scrambling out. Hoses unloaded. Hordes of spectators.) Yanking my arm, he tore me away from the mirror. I stumbled down the stairs with him, out into the cold, onto the street before the searching eyes of curious onlookers. Ah, but at least, I sighed, there were no curlers in my hair.

School Days

Smalltown introduced me, Marlane, Bro and L'il Bro, to an entirely new world of life experiences.

Marlane's blonde hair was fine and wispy when she was in Grade One. Yet she insisted my mother pull her strands into a ponytail. Except by the time we had walked to her Grade One class in the Old Town Hall, her wisps had escaped to fly around her cherub face. She never realized her ponytail had disappeared among dozens of bobby pins and coloured barrettes.

My Bro and I had to walk 5 km to and from the only elementary school in town on the other side of the railroad tracks. ("You live on the wrong side," came the taunt). Bro, small for his age, was constantly bullied and taunted by a couple of local boys. He lived in terror each school day. My Bro is a big guy now. No-one would dare assault him.

School discipline

I distinctly remember our Grade Five teacher. A man. Most unusual at that time. His voice boomed like the wrath of God and his eagle eyes scanned the room for truant behaviour.

During one of our many tests, most of the class -- except for goodie-goodies -- cheated. We wrote the answers on a small piece of paper, placed it beside us on our desk seats, our heads down so we could scan our cheat sheet at the same time we were writing.

Suddenly there was a mighty whack as Man Teacher smacked his book down atop his desk. We all stopped writing immediately, terrified at the Judgement Day explosion. He called up shivering Jamie, a small piglet of a boy who sat behind me. I could hear him whimpering as he slithered to the front of the class. "CHEATER!" yelled Man Teacher, pointing to Piggy Jamie.

At once there was a quiet rustle of cheat sheets shoved into desks. There was also a collective increase in heartbeats. Then Man Teacher ordered poor Jamie to open his hands. Each hand quivered. Man Teacher whacked Piggy five times on each open palm; with each whack tears sprang into Piggy's eyes. At this poor kid's expense, we all learned never to cheat again.

Little People

Little Lucy down the street was a child of incest. Her mother was her sister. It took me awhile to figure that one out but my best friend, Gayle, told me this was so.

Dumb Dougie, as we (cruelly) called him, sat on the front steps of his family's frame home, rocking his body, arms wrapped around his torso, singing to himself. Other kids nonchalantly called him 'strange' due to family in-breeding.

More than just a cornfield

The tall cornfield across the street was the perfect place to sexually explore yourself or your boyfriend. Deep in the heart of the patch was a flattened area with overhead intertwined cornstalks. The perfect hiding place. All kids knew about it. Today, I wonder whether the farmer suspected any improper shenanigans. He always left that patch fort intact.

A Mill and Blacksmith shop

The abandoned old Mill by the river was haunted. No-one dared venture inside this vacant decrepit building. Through its broken windows we could see massive spider webs between abandoned machines. We thought about the serious size of those spiders. And crimes that must have taken place there.

At a major corner on our side of the tracks was the blacksmith's shop. Now long gone, his was the best place to hang around on a cold winter day. Especially when he let you get close to his fire to thaw frozen fingers.

Back to the past

On the way back to our past, Marlane and I easily found our Main Street home. It still stood as we remembered it, minus the barn and loft where we often jumped into piles of hay below. My bro's rabbit hutch, built by my father and located next to the barn, contained one adorable brown-spotted rabbit that thrived on excess greens from my mother's garden, once the pride of the neighbourhood, as it thrived in nutrient-rich soil. Unfortunately – and a sign of today's world -- the present homeowners told us the soil in that spot is 'absolutely no good' for growing anything.

Saturday night dinner

Marlane and I fondly recalled the old wood stove in the large kitchen on which my mother created from scratch her traditional Saturday evening meal: homemade baked beans, homemade brown bread, homemade ice cream whipped with the cream that rose to the top of the bottled milk.

Fresh milk was delivered each day from neighbouring farms via the milk wagon; the wagon was drawn by an aging nag with bony growths on his joints, his mouth covered with a feed bag of oats so he could munch while lumbering numbly through the same route each day.

And then, there was the DOM with WHT

No-one warned me. I was the new city slicker girl who had to find out for herself. But I quickly learned about the DOM with WHT. Subteen girls in our Smalltown avoided this particular shopkeeper of a general store. His reputation had spread. He was the DOM (Dirty Old Man) with WHT (Wandering Hand Trouble), who was hungry for 'feeling up' subteen girls. DOM with WHT became the mantra among us grade-fivers. Our parents could never understand why we refused to go into his store alone.

You can go back

For Marlane and me, the visit to our past brought back some golden, some haunting, but forever vivid memories. We also realized you can go back and find the past even more fascinating through adult eyes.

- Published July 2022, in Story Quilt

Young Sexuality

Deftly he touched my blouse and expertly massaged my developing breasts. Then he winked and grinned...a stupid grin.

I was in grade five and the new girl. He was old man Gladstone, the fat, former mayor of this little town to which we had moved.

And right now I was alone in Gladstone's store. And terrified.

At once, two strong emotions swept over me. To my horror, I seemed to enjoy his touch! A zig-zag of delicious excitement hurtled around my body. Yet in my sane, innermost mind, I knew this was evil and wrong! Wasn't it?

Without moving a muscle, I looked straight ahead, my jumpy mind completely confused. I'm not certain but I think he said, "How lovely your breasts are, Pamela."

His big hands were still roving.

And then, still riveted in fear, he pressed his huge body against my small one. I felt his hardness rub against me while his hands flitted between my legs.

I didn't move. Then he spoke.

"Come and choose whatever sized cone you'd like... no charge." His steely blue eyes smiled patronizingly.

Somehow, I found myself out on the street with a triple butter pecan cone in my shaking hand and a hot dime in my pocket. My mother would be very surprised to learn I never spent that dime since I had nagged her for it all noon hour. She must have been puzzled, too, by my sudden behaviour of atonement. I remember insisting I wash our very large kitchen floor.

It took a long time before I told my best friend, Adele, about my experience in Gladstone's store. I was scared, ashamed, and perplexed at my reaction. I should have just slapped his face and run. Why did I stay? Because I was frightened! What if he told my parents? I cringed as I thought of my overly-strict father.

When I mentioned it to Adele, it was a hot, lazy afternoon and we were loafing in our barn loft hoping Danny and Gord would show up to wrestle. We were tough and could always beat those two.

"You ever - uh - have trouble with Gladstone?" Adele eyed me cautiously. I went on, slowly. "He ever - uh - feel you where he wasn't supposed to?" There. It was out.

Without hesitating, Adele rattled off "promise and cross your heart you won't tell anyone?"

"Promise and hope to die."

"He did."

Now that her secret was out, I shared mine with her. She was totally unimpressed.

"What did I tell you about him?" she gloated. "He's just a dirty old man!"

Our friendship bond grew stronger now. And so did my continuing education into the flavour of this 'quiet' town.

Still, I was ignorant. And I was concerned about what might happen to me because of Gladstone's dirty hands.

"Adele," I asked hesitatingly, "you don't have to worry about having babies because of him, do you?"

"Naw," she replied with a laugh. "You've got to do more than that!"

I laughed too. Then quickly asked, "were you excited? Scared? When it happened to you, I mean."

"Both...You?"

I nodded.

When Danny and Gord arrived, we played tag, and jumped from the loft, and climbed trees. They were really being used to relieve our boredom but that was all right. They were just boys.

Needless to say, I was terrified of Gladstone and only under the greatest duress and with someone else would I venture into his store. Whenever I passed him on the street he always winked. I hated him.

One fine end of summer day my mother ordered me to run to Gladstone's store. My baby brother was seriously ill and she wanted aspirin...immediately.

In the midst of the crisis, I forgot my fears. As I opened the door to Gladstone's the bell tinkled loudly. To my enormous relief Gord was also in the store buying candy and taking his pokey old time with it. I was overjoyed.

Behind those round spectacles of his, Gladstone stared at me greedily. I avoided his hungry glare.

"Aspirin please," I said.

I watched Gladstone disappear down the aisle.

Suddenly he waved at me from the far end. "Here, Pamela, it's right here!"

Because Gord was in the store, I never gave it a second thought. That was my mistake. Almost imperceptibly Gladstone stood behind me, touched my top and lightly caressed my breasts again.

I froze.

I heard him breathe heavily into my ear. "I'll get rid of Gordie."

I stood rooted to the spot, paralyzed. In the dim distance I heard him bribe Gordie with free candy. And then Gordie was gone.

Glued to the floor, I listened carefully as I heard the old hardwood floors squeak. I knew Gladstone was coming.

Quietly, carefully, I sneaked behind the counter to the door. Suddenly he was in front of me.

"I thought you needed aspirin, Pamela?" he smiled too sweetly.

"Please Mr. Gladstone," I pleaded. "My baby brother's sick and I've got to rush right home or my father (oh how I emphasized 'father') will come to get me and..." The old man was inching closer and closer. My heart was thumping louder and louder.

And then, just when I thought he'd get me, the back door of the store opened and in flitted Sparrow, Gladstone's spindly wife. How happy I was to see the skinny old lady and her pinched face!

I fled home, clutching the aspirin, my fear flying with me.

Then, slowly, I calmed and the fear subsided. Instead, there was that delicious chill thrill again--that longing to be touched again, that powerful emotion that confused and tormented and delighted me, all at once. My feelings were ambivalent, precarious, and very private.

All my life I hated that dirty old man.

1983 Review:

"Young Sexuality has story line and colour...."
- Irving Layton

Part 2

Exploring the World
with Uneasy Eyes

Heather and her husband have travelled much of the world. She has had many articles of her travels published in domestic and international publications. Here are some from that collection...

INDONESIA

THE DAY I ALMOST LOST MY HUSBAND IN THE INDONESIAN JUNGLE

So, what am I doing here in the sky…

…clinging to my scruffy looking seat in this small regional (Merpati Airlines, now defunct) propeller driven plane that uses a large Velcro strap to hold fast the exterior cabin door?

And what's that damp stain… is that rain seeping through the small window pane, sliding down the interior wall beside me?

I am hyperventilating, praying, willing a safe landing on this short flight from the mainland of Indonesia to Kalimantan, the Indonesian section of this giant, rugged island of Borneo. My husband, Norm, seated beside me, is asleep. Calm, relaxed, always ready for an adventure, his head flops back and forth as the plane dipsy doodles up and down. He does not know how close we are to not making our destination.

Gingerly, I glance around at our fellow passengers. Since we are independent travellers, I am always interested in spotting, and studying, others like us. I spy another twosome, a North American couple judging by their clothing, burrowing into guidebooks on Kalimantan/Borneo. The Indonesian guy across the aisle is reading a magazine. No-one, but me, appears concerned.

Why am I the only one so stressed?

Years ago, I used to be the reluctant traveller. But I've changed. Sort of. Sometimes. Partly it's because my husband and I have had some marvelously life changing --- a charitable word --- adventures on our world travels. Deep down inside, I knew I always wanted to experience my own unadulterated delight in exploring a culture other than my own. But it's taken me years to get to this acceptance stage. Meaning, I get it now. I can leave for uncharted territory without a bad case of culture shock, jittery nerves, and hysteria.

But I don't get this current situation we're in…flying on an out-of-date airplane in an area of the world where safety first does not seem the motto.

We've explored Indonesia for six weeks now. This forthcoming Kalimantan excursion is our final destination. We are heading for Tanjung Puting National Park and Camp Leakey, an Orangutan Recovery Station. Camp Leakey was founded by Canadian orangutan researcher Dr. Biruté Galdikas in 1971. The camp's name honours famed paleo-anthropologist Louis Leakey, who funded Galdikas' orangutan research. (Leakey also funded Jane Goodall's work with chimpanzees and Dian Fossey's studies with mountain gorillas. The three women became known as The Trimates, or Leakey's Angels.)

But before we get to meet our orangutan relatives, we hole up in Surabaya, East Java. From this city's airport we will fly to Kalimantan. Surabaya's lodgings depress me. Somehow, in a hot and sunshine-filled country, we manage to find this gloomy guest house: a vintage English-style home, its large windows covered and barred from natural light by heavy maroon velvet drapes; black wicker rocking chairs on a shaded back patio; army green moss trailing over a rocky protrusion into a sunken garden and pond blanketed with dark khaki algae.

At last, we arrive at the Surabaya airport, eager to move on, to study the orangutans at Camp Leakey. But first we must board our flight. The open concept airport is bustling: that familiar humid, sticky smell of the tropics is stifling. Large overhead ceiling fans do little to provide relief. My stomach butterflies are in full flight. We show our confirmed tickets at the counter.

"Sorry. No room," says the airline attendant.

"What? But we have confirmed tickets. Right here…." And we show our printed proof.

"Sorry. No room," the attendant says again as if we are deaf. "Next please!" We are unceremoniously given the bum's rush. We look around in disbelief, and then despair. Our flight to Kalimantan is leaving shortly.

Lucky for us (later I think not so lucky for us), one of our country contacts who drove us to the airport, has not left. He was waiting to make sure we made our flight.

Wide-eyed, we explain our predicament.

He says only one thing. "Do you have a plain white envelope?"

I'm slow to catch on. Norm is not.

"You mean a bribe?" when it finally dawns on me.

"These people do not make much money," says our contact matter-of-factly.

Norm stuffs the equivalent of $20 Cdn in the envelope, grabs our tickets and me again, says goodbye once more to our helper man, surreptitiously slips our envelope to the same counter attendant. As if we are VIPs, we are whisked through the gate to the waiting plane on the tarmac. One look at the seen-better-days plane and I'm sorry we've spent money on a bribe.

So here we are now: me, my husband, and a few other foolish/hardy souls, aboard this flight to the jungle. I continually eyeball the Velcro strap for fear it will snap. Praying it will hold that exterior door. And, what's this now? Rain! Well, this is a tropical country. Sudden rainfalls are common. But since when does rainwater seep into, and slide down, the interior wall of an airplane in flight?

Somehow, after a one-a-half-hour-hold-my-breath flight, we land --- safely --- and find ourselves in a seedy, damp smelling airport, the humidity ramped higher by the passing rainstorm. Our hotel is not far in this coastal jungle town of Pangkalan Bun, gateway to Tanjung Puting National Park and our orangutan venture.

Mishaps begin almost immediately. Our taxi, chugging along a muddy, pot-holed road to our hotel, breaks down. Our driver is exasperatingly apologetic, waving down possible replacements as they slosh by. I need to use a washroom in the worst way. Fetid smells mixed with steaming air are upsetting my fragile innards again.

At this moment I wonder, what am I doing here? On the other hand, my husband calmly accepts this as another sidebar to our adventure.

Finally, in an actually operating taxi, we arrive at our hotel, the Hotel Bahagia. 'Top rated' because each room has an attached *mandi* (bathroom), a frivolous detail I insist we include when finding accommodation in a jungle town. By this time, I am desperately in need of a mandi.

Bursting into the room, all looks fine…the usual accoutrements, bed, windows, wardrobe, mirror…but where's the mandi? I spy a door on the far side of the room, race across the bare floor, thrust open the door. And stop suddenly.

To get to the mandi, I must first manoeuvre down a few steps to a lower room. The odour from this area is most foul: sewage mixed with heat, humidity, mildew, tropical rot.

As if to remedy first impressions, dinner at the hotel that evening is pleasant because there are no surprises. Grilled shrimp --- plump, plentiful, perfect --- with rice. Always rice. Am beginning to hate rice.

The next morning, we begin our two hour --- seems much longer --- journey by motorboat to Tanjung Puting National Park and the Orangutan Rehabilitation Centre at Camp Leakey.

Our young male guide, Bayu (meaning Wind), is effervescent, accommodating, and knowledgeable. Of slender build, he offers us the only meal we will eat that day (although we do not know this at the time). Served cold, the two boxes come from his cache of items stowed beneath his driver's seat at the stern of the motorboat where potent gasoline fumes are profuse. We notice he does not eat.

Our cuisine is cold fried chicken, rice, gado gado (*mix-mix*), a traditional Indonesian dish of vegetables --- bean sprouts, tofu, cucumbers, all mixed in a spicy peanut sauce --- and bottled water. (By the end of this Indonesian adventure, where we lived almost exclusively on fish, rice and gado-gado, I refused any of these foods for months after our return to Canada.)

Bayu proves a knowledgeable English-speaking guide. With a genial smile that shows some missing teeth, he pronounces proudly: "On this (Sekonyer) river at night, we will see hundreds of monkeys, thousands of fireflies…" It's a phrase we still use to exaggerate any claims. He also conveniently forgot to mention zillions of mosquitoes.

Soon after our departure on this muddy river, the menacing sky launches its monsoon-like rains. We are drenched by this torrential downpour in the open speedboat. Bayu smiles and nods as he skillfully manoeuvres the boat through tangled jungle growth in the heavy deluge. At times there is no open water path, so, like Jungle Jim, he takes his machete and cuts a swathe through the overgrowth. Nonchalantly, he weaves his boat through this thick maze of wilderness. I keep watch for coiled snakes to drop down on us.

Finally, we arrive at Camp Leakey. Like a lucky omen, the hot tropical sun suddenly emerges to beat down and greet us. Now we are drenching in sweat.

As soon as Bayu docks, my husband, eager to finally see these People of the Forest, leaps from the boat to the long wooden boardwalk. I lag behind to take in a wider view of a low building at the end of the boardwalk surrounded by dense verdant bush. Then I hoist myself onto the walk.

That's when I notice a reddish-brown, life-size, lumbering orangutan. A female from the look of her *(Adult females weigh between 30 to 50 kg (66 to 110 lb.) and stand about one m (3.3 ft.) in height)*, she appears on the boardwalk from the surrounding jungle. Like a shy bride --- and studying us with curiosity --- she cautiously approaches Norm, who looks enraptured. She only has eyes for him. He only has eyes for her. Right now, my brain disengages, clicks into slow motion.

Languorously, she extends a long hairy arm towards him, as if to touch his hand in greeting. I can see he is thrilled with this gesture. He extends his. It is love at first sight.

I watch in awe as she curls those long, strong, human-like fingers around Norm's wrist and hand. In a trance it appears, he willingly grasps her hand in return. Gradually, slowly, still mesmerizing with her dark chocolate-coloured eyes, she begins to walk away with him. Like an odd couple, my husband and Jezebel stroll hand in hand; they veer off the ramp together towards the jungle. Little do I know my husband's calm demeanour is fading as he realizes her grip is iron-clad. She tightens her hold but doesn't hurt. There's no escaping her grip.

In my slow-motion mode, it appears she intends to take him with her, perhaps back to her nest. And it occurs to me at that moment, I might lose him. Forever. To a fearfully strong rival.

My mind flashes forward, entertains crazy thoughts. What will I tell our three sons…that their father chose an orangutan over me? Our youngest might think that's cool.

What will I tell our friends --- he left me for a female orangutan? One of them might rebound with 'was she sexy?'

What will I tell each set of parents? Norm's parents will be horrified. Mine, at least my artist father, might be intrigued with the possibilities from this surreal adventure.

Suddenly, as if in a jungle movie when the director yells CUT!, an assistant from the camp appears, races along the boardwalk from the low building. He yells at Jezebel, gestures wildly, waves his arms in excitement.

She turns and looks at him with soft, languid eyes.

The assistant speaks harshly in an Indonesian dialect to her. She looks confused. Her feelings are hurt. She suddenly releases Norm's hand. Backs shyly into the dense bush. We all watch in awe as she swings from tree branch to tree branch, disappearing from sight without a backward glance at her jilted lover. I stare at Norm. He stares back in disbelief, shakes his hand, as if to feel it's still there.

We will always remember this close encounter with Jezebel as the day I almost lost my husband in the Indonesian Jungle.

And I forgot my camera.

TUNISIA
ANOTHER DAY, ANOTHER SCAM

Canadiennse! Canadiennse! The old man calls out behind us in the Medina of Tunis.

He finds us again at another crowded, stuffed market à la Istanbul only not as large... but large enough to get lost in: filled with mazes, narrow alleyways, crowds of people, all with similar merchandise hanging in, around, and over the small stalls. Each one looks like the other. My husband had spoken to the old man earlier about the mosque, closed due to prayers.

You want to see the Panorama view on top? he asks.

We do. Big mistake.

Meandering alleys

Old man leads us through a honeycomb of a maze. Think I should be dropping crumbs along the way, like Hansel and Gretel. How else to find our way back should he decide to abandon us? We may have to bribe him to get us back.

Up and over, through and around, and yes, even passing into, and out of, a carpet stall he leads us. Finally, true to his word, we reach the precipice---the top---for a panoramic view of surrounding Tunis with its minarets and mosques. We marvel at the scene, take photos, explore the cemented area and all the while I'm thinking...how the hell are we going to find our way out of here?

Now he motions us to follow him down. Back to the medina entrance. I am silently relieved. My husband, I know, is prepared to tip him for his trouble. But there is no need.

Pressure to buy

Old Man leads us to his perfume oil stall where he insists we sit on stools as he delivers a lecture on the values of his merchandise including his BoomBoom oil for great sex.

Yep. It's another scam. So we pay into the obligatory scam-release fund (not for BoomBoom but for a rose fragrance) and get out of there faster than a magic flying carpet.

No Surprise

When I ask his name, I should have known already. *Ali.* Just like the first con artist the day before...!

Ali Story

As soon as our guide dropped us off at the Souk (a smaller version of The Grand Bazaar in Istanbul) in Sousse, Ali appeared by our side. I recognize you from the hotel, he said. I work there. My name is Ali. What are you looking for? Let me help you. You are very lucky. This is the final day of a three day fair and prices are very good... I can take you to a special place for leather.

We are not interested in leather. And although Norm and I can't say anything to each other because of his presence, we are both thinking the same thing... this guy is a scam artist.

Let me take your photograph, I said, *since you work at our hotel.*

Oh, please, no, madam, please wait until I am in uniform as I want to look professional.

And so we become unwilling participants as Ali leads us into the souk and through the narrow alleyways to....surprise, the shop of leather where a big 50% sign is there. *Madame must come and look at the coats. Monsieur must try one.*

We have no money with us, I said. *Everything's at the hotel.*

Well, no matter. We take credit cards or you can buy here and pay at your hotel.

Well, we just didn't fall off the eggplant truck yesterday. So we begged off, Ali disappeared, and if not for the fact we've been scammed in our earlier years, who knows? BTW, Ali doesn't realize it but I did get his photo with Norm.

MEXICO

BLOOD IN THE DIRT

The smell of fresh blood mingled with red dust wafts up my nose. As if to ward off the unwelcome stench, I close my eyes and begin to slow down my breathing.

This is my first ever bullfight in Mérida Mexico and I am not sure I want to be here. As we wind our way into the stands at *plaza de toros*, pushing through polite but determined animal activists who carry signs to abolish bullfighting, I realize not all Mexicans love this spectacle. Despite the opposition, there is part of me that wants to experience this slice of Mexican culture of Spanish origin.   I want to compare it with my memory of Ernest Hemingway's account of the *corrida de toros* in Death in the Afternoon.

My senses are on high alert.   The hot sun beats down mercilessly while around the bullring sit the spectators; some are families with small children. Higher in the circular stadium is a Mexican brass band.   Like any Saturday afternoon ballgame, vendors hawk *botanas* (snacks like french fries, hot dogs *con* chili, *tortas*—sandwiches, drinks, small toys, miniature matador capes).

On the announcement board is the weight (536 kg.) of the first bull, bred at an Uxmal ranch in the south of the Yucatán state. The band strikes up and a roar from the crowd announces the release of the black beast---a regal animal with mean curved horns--- decorated with the colours of the breeder on his back. This bull is angry and shows it.   Rocketing from the door marked *toril* he charges into the ring. He paws the dirt.   He snorts his disapproval. He is all energy, wound up like a clock and warily sizing up his surroundings.   He is beautiful and majestic.

First to work *El Toro* is the matador's assistant to give the matador an idea of how the bull reacts to certain moves.

Then come the *picadors,* two heavily padded men on heavily-padded blindfolded horses, whose job is to stab three sets of elongated lances into the bull's shoulders. *El Toro* is not amused and uncooperative. Head down, he charges one of the *picadors* who hastily dismounts and retreats to safety leaving the horse to take the bull's repeated gores. The horse goes down against the wall of the ring. The crowd holds its collective breath. From behind safe wooden barriers bolt costumed assistants to distract the bull from his current quarry. *El Toro* moves away from the downed horse. Miraculously, the heavily-padded horse scrambles to its feet, the *picador* leaps back onto the shaken animal and they leave the ring.

Next come the *banderilleros,* whose job it is to thrust two 75 cm long wooden spears (*banderillas)* with harpoon-like points decorated with coloured paper into the bull's back, preferably approaching the bull in a straight line and delivering the spears from a height. Watching, hypnotized, one wonders how much more torment *El Toro* can take. His coat glistens in the beating sun as he shakes his great head defiantly but with slightly diminishing energy. Despite the provocation, he is still regal.

Now, the matador takes over. With his embroidered sequined outfit dazzling in the sun like flashing gold nuggets, he is resplendent, confident. Throughout the first stages of the fight, he has studied the bull's movements. Now with his *muleta* (cape) and sword he begins the foreplay; as the *muleta* swirls and falls, teases and twirls, the matador shows his artistry.

This is the point of fascination; this is when the matador seduces the crowd. Now the classical form and passion of the bullfight come into play: the disciplined graceful movements of the matador, the swish of his *muleta* as *El Toro* passes under it, the arched back and quick movements of the slender fighter, the closeness and oneness attained by both bull and matador, the eye contact between man and beast, the dance of life and death. Captivating, mesmerizing. We know the bull will lose this dance but at what point and how? All eyes are trained on *El Toro bravo* and his flashy performing antagonist to whom he is magnetically drawn.

El Toro is exhausted now. Turning to face the crowd, the matador's deliberate move to ignore the beast is his taunting way of showing spectators he is the conqueror now. The crucial moment, The Suerte Suprema, is near. Before he can deliver the final blow, the matador must be sure the bull is standing with his four feet together so the sword can easily pass between his open shoulder blades. The eyes of man and beast connect, locking one another into a world of their own. Then, at the right moment, there is a sudden swift movement as the matador lunges forward.

Where a moment ago he was pawing the ground, now El Toro Bravo falters and falls, leaving a pool of dark liquid in the dirt, the only evidence of a valiant fight he has lost.

In what seems a moment later, the once-noble warrior is unceremoniously dragged from the bullring by mules, after which he is immediately butchered and his meat delivered to the poor. There are a total of six bullfights during an event, each one divided into three parts, the last part being the face-to-face fight, which ends with the death of the bull. Each bullfight takes no more than 15-20 minutes.

CHAMULA INDIGENOUS: LOST IN TIME

The women do not vote. They do not cut their thick black hair and do not wear make-up. They breastfeed their children for as long as possible and carry them in cloth slings. This is a patriarchal society. Families often have up to eight children or more. A child is born with the mongoloid birthmark, like Asians in other parts of the world, indicating a connection among the races despite their distant locations. Their diet is mostly vegetarian with little or no dairy products so they appear strong and healthy. Animals are raised for their skins and not their milk.

Birth dates are not recorded; birthdays are not celebrated. In their cemetery high on the hill outside their town of Chamula near San Cristóbal de las Casas in Mexico, wooden crosses bear only the date of death.

This group of indigenous people, descendants of the Maya, carry on in the ancient traditions of their ancestors and by choice, do not want to change. In their town they have their own customs: spiritual leaders who prepare for their one-year volunteer position for 14 years bear the expense of their service. Civic leaders, paid by the Mexican government which accepts the community's autonomy, are elected by men only who cheer or raise their hats for their favoured candidate. Opponents are victims of catcall whistles, sling shots or thrown objects like eggs.

The dress code is based on natural fabrics. Men wear tunics of black or white sheep's wool (depending on the season). Men work the fields or in the town or travel to the U.S. for transitory jobs. The women, who can be found all over Mexico selling their woven wares away from home three months at a time, wear distinct skirts of black, sometimes patterned, and brightly coloured hand embroidered satin blouses of purple and turquoise shades. In cold weather, they hug shawls around their shoulders while their feet are in the open sandals of their ancestors. They are most often seen with a small child in their cloth slings on their backs. Women do not wear make-up or jewellery; they do not cut their thick, black hair.

Both men and women do not want to be photographed and photography in their Church in Chamula is forbidden. Their religion is based on the ancient healing rituals of Maya adapted to their current needs.

Entering their church is a step into another time, another culture. There are no pews. Family gatherings and rituals are on the floor with lit candles. The floor is covered with fresh pine needles, changed frequently, so the fragrance mixed with that of hundreds of lit candles, is euphoria for the senses. Mirrors on the saints symbolize the reflection of the sun. As we slowly meander towards the altar, winding our way through and past families sitting beside rows of lit candles, we see a healer. She has clasped a hen's legs together and holding the bird upside down, she is passing the hen along the body of an ill person to rid him of evil spirits. The family has brought eggs, soft drinks (Pepsi or Coke, symbolizing black corn), and pox (pronounced posh) a hard liquor. String and percussion musicians play continuously at the side of the altar. Along with the heady scent of incense and continual chanting, the interior of the church takes on a mystical experience.

A wizened woman dressed in traditional dress accosts me as I carry the camera to take an exterior photo of the Church. She wags her bony finger and hisses at me: "No…no…no…" Frankly she unnerves me and I quickly hide my camera. (Later, I sneak back and take a photo from another angle.)

Local law enforcement is swift. Cells of the jail (for males) face outwards to the community so everyone can see who is in prison. Women do have private cells within the jail. Feeding the prisoner is left to the family or, sometimes, through the benevolence of the spiritual leader. Most of the crime is petty thievery but if an individual is jailed a third time, he/she is banished from the community. A serious crime, like a murder, means the Mexican police get involved.

It appears the Mexican government has allowed the Chamulans to live within their own rules and codes of conduct. The Zapatistas support their way of life and are seeking that right for other Indigenous peoples in their fight against the government.

Our guide César takes us to a neighbouring sect in Zincanatun, similar in origin but who developed in a slightly different direction. We visit a typical house of weavers. Beautiful tapestry. The women have their hair pinned up on top of their heads. We are told it's because they have washed their hair and they wear it that way until it has dried.

In this home we also watch corn tortillas being made by hand. We are offered freshly cooked ones to eat. Each tortilla is wrapped around an onion spike that was bought in the Chamula market. It is delicious.

Our group includes 7: one couple from Israel, one couple from Switzerland, and three Canadians.

CROSSING THE SIERRA MADRE RANGE AND LIVING TO TELL ABOUT IT

Background:

Sierra Madre, chief mountain system of Mexico, consisting of the Sierra Madre Oriental, the Sierra Madre Occidental, and the Sierra Madre del Sur form the dissected edges of the vast central Mexican plateau; a volcanic belt along the plateau's southern edge links the three sierras.

Extending from northwest to southeast through Mexico from the U.S. border, the rugged Sierra Madres, 6,000-12,000 ft (1,829-3,658 metres) high, with deep, steep-sided canyons (*barrancas*), have long been a barrier to east-west travel.

The terrain ranges from permanently snow-covered peaks to hot, tropical valleys; and from the humid, thickly vegetated seaward slopes to the dry, largely barren interior-facing slopes. Agricultural products vary according to the climate. Lumbering is done in the N Sierra Madre Occidental. The Sierra Madres have a great wealth of minerals including iron ore, lead, silver, and gold. The mountains are sparsely populated, with settlement limited to mining towns and farm communities.

The Sierra Madres hold good potential for hydroelectric-power development, and several stations have been built in the northern ranges.

The Sierra Madre Oriental, beginning in barren hills south of the Rio Grande, runs for about 700 miles (1,130 km) roughly parallel to the coast of the Gulf of Mexico, ranging from 10 to 200 miles (16-320 km) inland. It reaches an elevation of 18,700 feet (5,700 metres) in Citlaltépetl, which belongs also to the volcanic belt, Cordillera de Anáhuac.

This belt, which divides Mexico in half at about lat. 19° N and includes the peaks Popocatépetl and Iztaccihuatl, on the other end joins the Sierra Madre Occidental. This range, paralleling the Pacific coast for c.1,000 mi (1,610 km), extends SE from Arizona. Its main escarpment is more abrupt than that of the eastern cordillera. From c.5,000 ft (1,520 m) in the north, elevations reach over 10,000 ft (3,048 m) in the south.

The Sierra Madre del Sur is a tumbled, broken mass of uptilted mountains that touch the Pacific coast but form into no clearly defined range. It spreads over South Mexico between the volcanic belt and the Isthmus of Tehuantepec and forms the natural harbor of Acapulco.

And now the bus ride…..

When we leave our small comfortable hotel in Oaxaca, it is 6:00 a.m. and we aren't aware of the hair-raising drive ahead of us over the Sierra Madre Mountains to Puerto Escondido. We eat no breakfast and not until later do we realize this is good planning for we are embarking on a 6 ½ hour drive through extreme terrains.

At 6:30 a.m. we join other passengers in a small white Ford minivan that can carry 18. Sitting directly behind the driver so we can see what he's doing--or not doing--we strap ourselves in with a safety belt but not sure why. Plunging over a cliff will make no difference.

Our driver is a jovial Mexican who talks incessantly for four continuous hours into his hand-held CB radio while steering with one hand, lurching around drop-dead hairpin curves and switchbacks over bumpy roads with no guard-rails that fall straight down for thousands of feet. His chatter even drowns out the loud Mexican music coming from the radio. I feel vomit coming…

Our driver has a strong faith since the dashboard is heaped with sets of rosary beads, pictures of protective saints, and other religious paraphernalia.

On the mountain road, donkeys, burros, goats and/or cattle stroll casually and carelessly along the outcroppings, vying with our van for space.

Norm pulls his famous act and falls asleep during this ride of terror. Unbeknownst to him he is tossed from side to side as the van lurches around each precipitous corner. It is good he is strapped in as he flips from one side to the other, then flops back, like a ping pong ball. Flip. Flop. Flip. Flop. It's almost comical if it wasn't for the fact the flips and flops are caused by twists and turns along the precarious route.

Finally, after 4 ½ hours of straight driving up, up, and just over, our driver stops for breakfast and a washroom break. His choice of restaurant and washroom facilities matches his penchant for driving. We are parked on an undersized projection of land that leans over a long drop. *El restaurante* does not look clean for our poor jumbled and pristine gringo stomachs. We decide we will not eat while the Mexicans order with gusto.

The washroom facilities, if that's what you can call them, are inadequate and not so clean. The buildings sit on the edge of the outcropping and hide two seatless and stained toilets (no surprise), one for each sex. Flushing is pouring a pail of water into the toilet. Let's not guess where the toilet contents go.

While the others eat and we stroll around (not too close to the edge), we hear what sounds like Andean flute music. We listen intently but because the road is nothing but curves we cannot see the music's source. Suddenly around the bend comes a small white car. The music we hear is the jingly song of an ice cream truck. Lo and behold, in the middle of the mountains in the middle of nowhere, we see an ice cream truck. Our mouths hang open in amazement, the ice cream truck does not stop… it just heads on down the mountain road.

Unfortunately, what we could not see on the van during our early morning departure we can now see very clearly. Bald tires. Three of them. The fourth, with a slight tread, is on the back right hand side of the vehicle.

More discoveries await us after the rest stop. Careening around the road, our driver suddenly screeches to a halt. On another outcropping on the side sits a parked station wagon. It looks like it's been in an accident. *MachoMan* driver instructs his sidekick to get out and look over the edge to look for any bodies, or remains. *El sidekick* peers over the ridge, looks back at his boss driver, and shakes his head. Okay, no bodies, then let's get going. We are off again.

Finally, we arrive at Puerto Escondido, the surfer's paradise on the Pacific coast of Mexico. We are both ready--me especially--for a stiff drink.

We toast our unbridled joy at having survived this harrowing minivan journey, of course.

But most of all, we toast the virtues and expertise of our driver.

INSIDE A MAYA FAMILY COMPOUND

In his cupped hands he holds a baby turkey, a *poult,* only a few weeks old. It has a piece of red wool drawn through the skin on the top of its head which stands up, as if the poult sports a modern hairstyle.

"This red string is to ward off evil spirits and keep the baby turkey healthy," says Abel who lives in this Maya family compound. "Only four out of ten baby turkeys will survive."

We are guests inside Abel's family compound located in Santa Elena, a Maya village along the Ruta Puuc (hilly route) in the southern part of Yucatán state in Mexico. Abel is one of eight in a family still led by his father, 72, and his mother, 62. Numerous other relatives, including Abel, his wife and two children, live there. The International Women's Club of Mérida is supporting an awareness initiative focusing on the needs of these people.

The Maya have a history of about 3000 years in the Yucatán Peninsula. Today, just as in ancient times, their basic food source is corn. Abel explains how the very dry and colder than unusual fall season has taken its toll. Corn production was reduced by more than 30 percent; honey production reduced by over 40 percent. "60 percent of the people in Santa Elena work in the honey industry," he says. No rain meant corn plants shrivelled; fewer flowers and cold temperatures "kept the bees in the hives" living on their own honey. With no product to sell while still forced to buy corn for tortillas and poultry feed, the proudly independent people of Santa Elena are facing an economic crisis.

The Maya compound is built on bare earth surrounded by a carefully and artfully constructed wall of loose stones and rocks, a staple of the Yucatán countryside. Abel invites us into his functional oval-shaped Maya home constructed of stone and stucco with a roof of palm fronds (*palapas*). The traditional Maya house is a single room with rounded corners, no windows, and one central door built to face east.

"My father built our home 57 years ago," he says with justifiable pride, "and the roof has only been replaced twice." A hammock hangs from the poles and beneath our feet, the earthen floor. It won't be long, though, before the earth floor is replaced by cement thanks to a federal government project.

It also won't be long before the traditional Maya home will be a reminder of the past, however. Abel mentions that each year 400 villagers head to the US as migrant farm workers and each year they return with new ideas for modernizing their homes.

We move on to the cooking hut adjacent to the Maya home where Abel's female relatives are cooking tortillas on a flat grill set over rocks. After removing them from the heat they are dusted with salt. Rolled like a cigar, warm tortillas are offered as a tasty reminder of our visit. Corn tortillas, prepared in the traditional way, are delicious! Hollowed out large gourds from the garden are used to keep the tortillas warm while smaller gourds are used as drinking cups set on a holder of intertwined vines. Every possible gift from nature is used.

We walk to the laundry shelter (*batea*). Ashes from the cooking fires are placed in buckets of water to soften the hard water native to this area. Then clothes are individually pounded and washed on a table-high stone counter with lots of elbow grease and a hard bar of soap. A shower is a bucket of water poured over the body along with a solid scrub of soap suds. In an environment of mostly earth, the older women are adorned in snow-white *huipiles* (traditional dress) edged in embroidered brightly coloured patterns while younger members favour western dress.

Roaming turkeys, chickens, pigs, and puppies share the earthen compound. Pigs are highly valued and when ready for market, word spreads quickly throughout the village. Often a piglet is given to another family to encourage self-sufficiency. Turkeys fattened on corn and tortilla dough provide added income.

Every other day or so, members of the family take their three-wheeled bicycle cart out to a nearby forest to collect wood for cooking. This is their only source of fuel and if you have driven into the Yucatecan countryside, you can see their neat bundles of wood piled onto the carts by the side of the road.

When there is corn to harvest, the family picks and shucks the dried corn kernels. In the morning the women take a bucket of corn kernels to the local tortilleria in exchange for masa (corn flour) resulting in those delicious tortillas. Kernels are no longer ground by hand because even the smallest village seems to have its own tortilleria.

As he moves about the compound, Abel is obviously proud of his Maya heritage and of the independence of his people. They are warm and welcoming and as curious about us as we are of them. To get over the current economic slump, however, they can get by with a little help from their friends.

LOVE HOTEL

(Tuxtla Guitérrez, capital city of Chiapas, Mexico)

We both hear the buzzer. Since we ordered room service (the only way to get food here), we assume our lunch is being delivered.

The buzzer urgently buzzes again so my husband rushes to open the garage attached to our room. The room door opens into the garage where he now hurries to press the red button to open the garage door. Suddenly I whisper loudly: "the window. You have to go to the sliding window!"

We are in one of Mexico's many love hotels where everything is circumspect but where you have to learn how to order food and what to do next. When you rent one of these *habitaciones/* rooms, you rent absolute discretion. These are rooms priced by the hour. It costs $25 Cdn dollars for eight hours with breakfast included for overnight guests.

No names are needed for registration. You drive your car into the adjoining garage, close the door, and receive your meals ordered by telephone via a discreet curtained and sliding window (like a fast food takeout counter) hidden behind a mirrored barrier. The waitress cannot see whether or not you are dressed as she places your food tray on the counter inside the sliding window. After payment (cash is best in these circumstances), she quickly disappears ready to serve her next client. She carries a two-way radio ready to tend quickly to the needs of other like-minded customers.

The spacious clean and pleasant room has radio, television, and heavy window curtains dominated by a king-size bed facing a large mirror that unfortunately slightly distorts and widens your image. On either side of the bed are two small rugs, one of Superman and the other of a Disney cartoon car. Overhead pot lights are on dimmers.

The furniture has fake wooden drawers and cabinets that do not open (you're only staying a few hours, right?) The sky-lit baño with marble floors features an indigo bidét and toilet, white fluffy towels and a multi-person size shower. The toilet tissue is scented to make sure your fragrance is desirable. Mints are discreetly left near the bed so your breath always smells kissing sweet.

There is no such thing as Internet (why would you bring a laptop to a love hotel?), only adult programming and movies.

The exterior has well-manicured shrubs and a flowering bush pruned in the shape of a heart. We are in a concealed room far from the maddening crowd in a hotel chain that protects its clients who check in for a few comfortable hours of private delight. No-one knows you are here and the proprietors could care less who you are or what your name is. It's easy to visualize a sensual Latino lover whispering sweet nothings into the ear of his or her hot partner while slowly disrobing to the throbbing music on the radio.

To start off our stay here, we order a bottle of white wine, comfort food like fried chicken, french fries and a salad (I am tired of Mexican food) ignoring other specialties like garlic shrimp and beef filet with black pepper.

When we finish our meal, my husband calls the *oficina* asking for someone to take away the dirty dishes. Something must have been lost in the translation, however, because when the buzzer sounds again and he opens the discreetly curtained sliding window behind the mirrored barrier, we receive a large plate of french fries.

As for the rest of the night, we leave that to your imagination.

MAYA HEALER

What was a white woman traveler doing before a religious altar in a little Mayan hut in a small Yucatecan village in Mexico with a strange man?

While staying at a nearby pueblo, I heard about a special Maya holy man who was a healer and source for spiritual purification. I needed his services. A taxi driver took me to his small, unpretentious Maya home because finding his place on my own in a maze of winding roads would be difficult.

When I first met Juan de la Cruz Pech of Temozón, I was struck by his gentleness, calmness and the sparkling friendliness in his brown eyes. They seemed wise and able to take me in all at once, looking into and through me. An elderly Maya woman wearing a blue embroidered *huipile* (traditional dress) was his first patient. She was suffering from arthritis and I watched as he treated her with his hands, herbs and melodic chanting.

Then it was my turn. He asked my name, writing it down. Gently, he took my hands, turning them palm side up, studying them and asked in Spanish: "*Dolor*"? Pain? I shook my head and explained in rudimentary Spanish I was seeking contentment, inner peace, a release from stress. He nodded. Then he carefully lifted my hands again and felt my pulse, not in the manner of a western medic, but instead, holding his fingers firmly on the veins of my wrist, listening intently to my inner workings. With a captivating, reassuring smile, he nodded again.

Collecting a sprig of herbs (I detected the fragrance of basil), he began his ritual. Lightly, he tapped my forehead, the top of my head, back of my neck and shoulders, down my arms to my hands, down my legs to my feet, waving away disharmony with the bouquet. At the same time he was chanting in Maya in a soothing, sweet tone. Incense drifted in all directions. I stared at his altar of fresh flowers that held images of Jesus, the Virgin Mary and Our Lady of Guadalupe, the patron saint of Mexico, along with unlikely items like a watch and a clock; I felt a rush of blood flush my face.

For fifteen to twenty minutes, the gentle elder touched, tapped, patted, and laid his hands upon me, especially around my head and neck. At times he deftly, delicately applied herbal salves and unknown potions, one from a small seashell. At one point I could smell pine. Finally, he led me to a hammock in which to lie and relax while he dabbed a herbal solution in my eyes.

I'm still not sure whether it was all in my mind, but at the end of my session, I was grateful to the soothing Mayan healer for his gift of inner peace and oneness with the universe that lasted at least three days … until it was time to re-enter the rat race.

IN THE HOUSE OF THE RISING SUN

It is 3 a.m. The alarm clock buzzes, breaking us out of a sound sleep. We are tired Canadians grabbing some warmth in

Progreso, Mexico, and this morning is the First Day of Spring. It's also the day, we are told, that we can witness a phenomenal sight: the sun rising on the Spring Equinox through the two windows and doors of a small temple, the Temple of the Seven Dolls, at a nearby Mayan archeological site. Those lucky enough to be touched by the sun's rays at this time are blessed with energy and good health.

In need of spiritual recharging, my husband and I decide we must experience this spectacle.

Sunrise is 6:10 a.m. The gates to Dzibilchaltun, where the temple is located, open at 4 a.m. The stars shine brightly and a waning moon still sheds considerable light. The night is calm and clear and magical already.

We race along the highway to our destination. Dzibilchaltun (meaning "place with writing on flat stones") contains almost 8,000 structures within its 19-kilometre area. This Maya city is one of the most important archeological sites in the Yucatecan Maya world.

The Temple of the Seven Dolls, one of the most impressive ruins, was so named for seven clay dolls with moveable limbs found buried there. Each doll has a different physical defect, suggesting that the temple may have been used for healing ceremonies. The structure is far from dramatic or awesome. Unlike other pyramids we've seen, it's unexceptional. Its claim to fame is its precise astronomical orientation: the doorways are arranged to mark important calendar dates.

The rising sun casts its rays precisely through the eastern door in the threshold of the western door on the Spring and Fall equinoxes, while the moon does the same on the last full moon before Easter Sunday.

At exactly 4 a.m., the gates swing open and we're pleased to find we are among a handful of early arrivals. Like pilgrims, we walk along the ancient road in the moonlight toward the temple. It is a mystical experience. Those walking in front and behind us walk silently. There is no sound save those of the night: the hoot of a pygmy owl, the gentle rustling of leaves.

Ahead stands the temple, its outline visible in the light of the starry sky.

Little by little, more people arrive. They creep along silently and speak in whispers, spreading out on the ancient road behind us.

We reach a low structure more or less in front of the temple. A set of a dozen or so steps, constructed thousands of years ago, leads to the top. We sit on the middle steps facing the temple.

It is now 4:45 a.m.

Others settle in, around, beside, below, behind, and above us. The growing crowd is quiet as we collectively listen to the night sounds and watch the stars in the bright sky.

We wait and watch the sky for signs of dawn.

And we wait.

Gradually, a pink colour washes the horizon behind the temple. We all sigh in unison. We know that once the sun, known by the Maya as the god Kin, appears, it will rise quickly. The opportunity to be caught in its rays---and be blessed, healed and energized---is not long. There is a precise moment when the rays light up the interior of the temple and touch the onlookers.

Slowly at first, the rays of the sun begin to flicker through the temple. From the bottom, the rays beam directly through the doors and windows---and the light is blinding. And then the rays completely fill and brilliantly light up the temple's rooms, bursting through its doors and windows that are now alive with glowing light.

Suddenly, the sun's rays touch us. We shiver with excitement.

Calm descends, then peace, and finally, a reverent appreciation follows: that we can be here, at this moment, in this special place, observing a phenomenon of Nature harnessed by ancient people who stood here in wonder and awe in the same way thousands of years ago.

SWEATING IN A MAYA SWEAT LODGE

Sweat is pouring from my pores. I am saturated with my own perspiration. My hair is wet and stringy. My breathing is laboured because of burning lungs and I am thankful we are in total blackness since I am struggling to sit upright. My instinct is to lie down in the fetal position on the floor where the air may be cooler and not so fire-hot. The steady beat of the drum haunts me with its rhythmic thump.... thump... thump. How long have I been in this temazcal and can I last this session of 45 minutes?

The name Temazcal comes from two Nahuatl words: *temas* for bath and *calli* meaning house. The temazcal is shaped like an igloo and represents the womb of Mother Earth. With a personal guide, Roberto, I have opted for detoxification and rebirth through this unique spiritual journey practised in similar ways by indigenous people worldwide.

On the day of the temazcal I eat lightly. Wearing only loose clothing (nudity is best but sadly our society is different from the ancients) and apprehensive about the coming experience, I begin. Just before entering the womb, I have an energy drink of cucumber, carrot and chaya (a favourite leafy green vegetable of the ancient Maya with more nutritional properties than spinach). Roberto performs the preparatory rituals: repeating my name, he scatters incense in the four cosmic directions, north, south, east and west representing the four elements of life, earth, water, wind and fire. Then he passes a bouquet of chamomile (for tranquillity) around me to enhance my spiritual cleanliness and detoxification process.

I am cautiously excited about this venture. Others have warned I must be in excellent health to endure the high temperatures of the temazcal. Was I? Medical researchers* report the body temperature during a sweat bath can rise to 40 C/104 F resulting in increased blood circulation and a faster more intense heartbeat that promotes the release of toxins from the body. Apparently every litre of sweat lost in a temazcal equals a full day's work by the kidneys. Immediately before entering the temazcal, I utter the words *In Láak' Kech to welcome the brotherhood of man as we merge into one. Then I chant A Láak' Kin to seal the greeting. These two phrases should be used each time I wish to speak while inside: the first to ask permission, the second to grant that permission.*

On my knees, I crawl through the small opening facing south into the womb of Mother Earth. The opening is known as "the pathway of the dead", so-called because we progress inevitably towards death from our moment of birth. Our journey represents the duality of life: mother and father, good and evil, life and death.

Once inside, I creep clockwise in a circle, from left to right, following the path of the planets in our solar system. Sitting cross-legged on a towel with musical instruments and a sprig of basil (for circulatory assistance), I notice a bouquet of rosemary and thyme hanging from a small hole in the roof. Though I'm still able to see, I know the light will soon be gone.

Hot lava rocks, heated in an external furnace that faces east where our father, the Sun, rises, are now introduced into the centre well. Their placement within the womb symbolizes the moment of conception.

Finally the door and rooftop opening are closed and a new cultural experience begins. I sit in pitch black space. Hot steam hisses loudly as herbal water splashes on the rocks. Roberto asks why I am here. Soaking with perspiration already, I mutter I seek a mystical journey through detoxification and a renewed appreciation of Mother Earth's life-giving gifts. Drum beats, herbal essences, the all-encompassing darkness, my own chanting and intense sweating, soon lift me to another dimension. And so my rebirth and detoxification begins:

Earth is my body

Water is my blood

Wind is my breath

Fire is my spirit

ANGELS TO THE RESCUE

"Guess what?" he says in shock. *He* is my husband and current driver of a rental van.

"What?" we echo simultaneously. *We* are me and four travel-weary visiting family members in the packed van on the busy *quota* (toll) freeway in the middle of a very hot (over 35 C) day in the Yucatán peninsula of Mexico.

"I think I'm out of gas," he says calmly as he steers the dying vehicle to the narrow shoulder edging the busy highway in the midst of construction. We're only halfway to our destination.

"What?" everyone cries in unison. "How can that be?"

Our driver explains. "I *thought* the rental agent said the car was gassed up. Now I think she said, the car *needs* to be gassed up. That's the problem when you don't speak the language."

A chorus of groans erupts.

Dicey Situation

Together -- except for the two teens -- we assess the situation. The teens are more interested in taste sampling the on-board Mexican snacks and peering at their screens. Besides, it's the adults who get to worry about these things.

Hmmm.

We really are sitting ducks. Having read all the mad media reports about violence in Mexico, one of our first-time visiting adults is kind of freaking out.

On the other hand, my husband and I are not. We've become familiar, unfortunately, with this toll road and its 'under construction' hazards. Although this dilemma has nothing to do with that.

Dire thoughts dash through worried heads: what if we're accosted by roaming thugs? How do we get help? Will anyone stop to help? Do we want anyone to stop? These and other catastrophic thoughts help fuel The Big Anxiety.

Meanwhile, traffic screams by: double tractor-trailer trucks that leave a residual hurricane swirl of hot air. One can only imagine being hit by one of these monsters. Game over.

Call for help

In Mexico, there is a federally funded highway service called The Green Angels (*Angeles Verdes*). The bilingual crew patrols the country's toll roads every day in green trucks to help motorists-in-need. The Mexican Tourism Ministry operates a fleet of 275 Green Angel pickup trucks with a service similar to our North American Automobile Associations.

Norm and I remembered the Green Angels from previous trips. We always carried their toll-free number. Using his limited Spanish, Norm called the Green Angels number. There appeared to be some language difficulty but finally, he was able to communicate our dilemma and position. He understood the Angels provide roadside assistance EXCEPT for gasoline. After all, who would drive anywhere without a full tank of gas?

Luckily, the despatcher said he would instruct a nearby Angel to deliver a container of gas. He should be at our location in about half an hour. (He probably got off the line and shook his head at the wisdom of some gringos…)

Quick decision

With rising temperatures -- inside and outside the van – plus increased *doble doble* truck traffic and late afternoon shadows soon to shift from early evening to pitch blackness, we waited. Snacks ran out. Tempers flared. Irrational fear increased…

A van of highway construction workers did stop… *what's the problemo*? they asked in Spanish.

"No gas," we admitted sheepishly.

They laughed. Not to be mean but with the realization our problem was not one with which they could help. So, they waved harmoniously and drove on.

"Let's call Carmen." Our landlady. "She should know what's happening to us and maybe has a faster idea."

The Rescue

At Carmen's request, (she also connected with the Green Angels), we took a screen shot of our GPS location plus photos of our stranded vehicle, forwarding both to her. "I will send Carlos (her husband) with gas." Due to her speedy reaction, we're convinced Carmen is related to The Road Runner.

The Green Angel

Suddenly, across the divided highway from us, we notice a truck has stopped. It is a Green Angel! Unfortunately, the *autopisto* is separated by a cement partition plus an additional high wire mesh permanently fixed atop the partition. Obviously meant to prevent any shenanigans: like crossing from one side to the other. This earthly obstacle does not stop our Angel.

Looking both ways, he first throws over the can of *gasolino*. It hits the road on our side. Then we watch in awe as he follows, catapulting his short, chunky frame over the top mesh webbed partition, landing safely on our side.

Before we know it, he has the hose from the can in our gas tank. We sigh with relief. And we pay him 260 pesos (about $20 Cdn) for the cost of the gasoline only.

The Silver Angel

Suddenly our attention is drawn back to the opposite side of The highway. A silver Kia has pulled up behind the Green Angel truck. It is Carlos, beloved husband of Carmen. When he sees the Green Angel, he shouts loudly to us between roaring-past trucks, that he will drive on to where the toll booth is, turn around, and come to our rescue, too.

Green then Silver

The Green Angel finishes and removes his gas hose. Shakes hands all around. We thank him profusely. He waves goodbye. Then, he reverses his actions. Looks both ways. Safe enough. Throws over the now-empty gas can to the other side. Then hoists himself up and hurls over the high webbed partition, landing miraculously again on his feet beside the empty gas can. Waves again. And he's off.

Silver Angel

Then, Carlos, our Silver Angel, pulls up behind us. He whips out his pocket knife, slices an empty plastic pop bottle lengthwise to use as a funnel and proceeds to add more gas to our tank. Once he's emptied his canister, he jumps into his car and follows us for awhile. Just to be sure we are okay.

Really?

In foreign countries, including Canada and U.S., news media outlets warn of danger and death in Mexico.

Really.

However, we can personally vouch that along the major highways in the Land of the Tamale in the Yucatán, we found Angels.

Really.

NEVER DRIVE AT NIGHT IN MEXICO

It was a dark and stormy night. Isn't that how most suspense dramas begin?

Only this night -- the one I'm writing about -- was only dark. Not just dark but pitch black – the kind of black that sets your nerves on edge because you can't see anything.

Missing the turnoff

We were driving 'home'-- that is, to Valladolid from Mérida in the Yucatán -- at night. A two-hour drive along the toll *(cuota)* road that used to be easy but no longer. With the ongoing construction of the new Maya train that follows the toll road route, the once fairly fast and smooth highway has become an obstacle course of construction. Mind you, we didn't do ourselves any favours. Darkness comes early this time of year even in the Yucatán; we didn't give ourselves enough time to drive back to Valladolid in the light.

As darkness descended, so did our uneasiness. One of the first cardinal rules in Mexico for foreigners is: Never drive at night. Thundering trucks pulling double trailers (*remolques dobles*) suddenly emerge from behind portions of highway cement barriers that separate two-way traffic, headlights blazing, roaring inches by our car. Said car is our neighbour's Kia that he rented to us. Right now, he is probably wondering about the safety of his vehicle in the hands of a couple of foreigners.

"Watch for the sign to Valladolid," cautions Norm, my husband, hunched over the steering wheel squinting through the windshield "…I'll concentrate on the road."

Of course, we (I) can't see any signage. Double trailer trucks ahead of us, beside us, around us, make peering into the blackness difficult, almost dangerous. Especially with their blinding headlights/tail-lights/side panel lights.

The Blue Dot is moving

Since we can't see any landmarks, I follow our progress via the GPS on our cell. The blue dot (us) is moving. But I still can't determine the exit to Valladolid except that we are moving towards it.

Suddenly, Norm utters a low groan. Between clenched teeth, he mutters, "I think we just missed the exit." As we stream past the truck that veered off to the right, I barely catch sight of a mini sign:'Valladolid' inconveniently stuck on the off ramp.

"Aaaagh!" I reply in anguish. "You're right. Only saw it after the truck pulled ahead!"

The Blue Dot is Not Moving

Something wrong with our GPS? I should have seen the exit coming. Glancing at the blue dot on our cell GPS, I see no movement. "No connection," I mumble. "We must be out of range."

Meanwhile, Norm continues to fight ongoing night blindness from oncoming truck headlights. Beyond their brightness, blackness covers the land and sky like a dark blanket.

No visible stars.

Getting off the next exit to return in the opposite direction is impossible. There are no exits. Just one continuous black ribbon of narrow asphalt with oncoming traffic on one side and construction barriers on the other.

Glancing at our cell, I see the blue dot moving again but it shows we are far past our turnoff. We are heading towards Cancun, a two hour drive away.

"Um," I venture. "We're going to Cancun."

Prolonged silence.

"Maybe we should spend the night there?" I suggest, "instead of driving back on this dangerous road?"

"That's ridiculous. I'd turn around but there's nowhere to do that," he says, as we continue to hurtle along the highway in the dark: orange fluorescent construction barrels on one side and oncoming blinding lights on the other. "Can't believe there aren't any exits or a place to turn around....I'll keep watching…"

Abruptly, hands on the wheel ready to turn, he says: "Here's a place. No oncoming traffic…."

"NO!" I panic scream. "BIG drop on this side!"

And so our hellish night drive continues towards Cancun, farther and farther away from Valladolid. No place to exit. No place to pull a u-turn.

And, like a heavy velvet curtain covering a window, the sky remains black.

The Blue Dot is closer

Once more, I glance at the cell…watch the moving blue dot as it continues its progress to Cancun. The resort city is closer now than if we turn around and drive back to Valladolid.

Suddenly, without warning, Norm pulls a u-turn in the middle of a wider, semi-lit construction zone with no oncoming or following traffic.

I hold my breath.

He did it! We are now heading back to Valladolid… despite the night blindness and the distance!

I follow the blue dot now like a cat watching a mouse. It is moving closer and closer to Valladolid. So we strain our eyes watching for the exit. We must not miss it this time.

"Here!" we both shout.

At last, we are on the overpass, only visible from the highway below by headlights on the bridge.

Finally…we are on familiar roads. And then, back in our Valladolid *casa.* And it's only 7 p.m.!

Much later, exhausted, we sit outside on a bench in front of our *casa* under the canopy of a starlit sky. Someone must have punched holes in that black velvet curtain.

No matter. We are safely back, sipping a smooth mezcal and solemnly swearing to follow our own advice: foreigners should never drive at night in Mexico.

OUTFOXING THE AIRPORT TAXI

The airport in Mérida, Mexico, is small, not too crowded, and arriving international passengers are quickly processed. In contrast, the Cancun airport is larger, more crowded, and often agonizingly slow to handle arriving passengers who wait in long lines.

Our destination is Valladolid, an inland historical city of the Yucatán Peninsula, that sits halfway – two hours -- between Mérida and Cancun. Comparing both airports, it makes sense for us to fly into Mérida: we even save a few hundred dollars on airfare.

To save even more money, we want to use a taxi driver familiar with Valladolid. We know a few taxi-drivers in that area and they know us. They are fair and helpful, and in return, we support them

However, using a Valladolid taxi in a Mérida airport is not a reasonable solution. Licensed airport taxi owners have paid high fees for the privilege of driving you to wherever. Their costs are passed along to the customer of course. To circumvent this problem, my husband Norm texted his Valladolid taxi driver before leaving Canada to discuss another airport pick-up possibility. Our man on the ground recommended -- and put us in touch with -- *Julio,* his compatriot taxi-driver in Mérida. It is agreed. Julio will pick us up at the airport. He will also charge a more reasonable fee, and transport us to our destination in Valladolid.

But wait! Julio's taxi is NOT authorized to enter the airport. However, he explains via a Spanish language text, we need only walk one kilometre and he'll meet us outside the airport.

Norm texts back (thank goodness for Google Translate) that this plan will not work for us. We have too much luggage to drag for 1 km.

Okay, texts back Julio in Spanglish, not to worry. He will drive another car into the airport visitor parking lot, pick us up with our luggage, drive to a designated spot outside the airport where we'll change cars, jump into his taxi, and be on our way.

We agree to this plan of action.

The time is at hand. We land on schedule. Quickly processed, we claim our luggage, use the washroom (a two hour car drive awaits us) and proceed to the exit. All the while, Norm is in text touch with Julio.

Outside the terminal now, we must find Julio. Lots of folks are standing around and they all look the same. How do we find Julio? Where to look? Norm hears the familiar ping of his cell. He reads a single command from Julio: *llámame*. Call me.

Immediately Norm does so. I hear two loud and brief exchanges. Suddenly there is a friendly wave in the crowd. And a wave back from us.

"Julio!" we grin.

"Welcome! *Bienvenidos*!" grins Julio, his arms outstretched in a warm greeting. "Let's get your bags into the car now!" He is a muscular man with thick black curly hair, a generous grin, and the air of a man in a hurry.

Together, Julio – and we – drag our luggage across the road under the watchful and suspicious eyes of waiting authorized taxi drivers.

He stops at the first row of parked cars. A sad-looking clunker of indeterminate colour, with junk shoved inside the trunk and piled on the back seat, greets us. Lest we show any concern, Julio is on top of it. "Don't worry," he says in broken English. "This is only until we get to my taxi." We smile conspiratorially.

And so we are off. Driving out of the airport like smug schoolchildren who think they have fooled a teacher whose back is turned.

Exiting the airport, we proceed along a wide avenue. Tall palm trees, uneven pavement, barbed wire-cement walled businesses greet our eyes. No other taxi is in sight.

"Do not worry!" he assures in Spanglish. "My taxi is not far on a side street with my friend." He must have seen us glance surreptitiously at each other.

Finally, he turns a corner, stops behind another car.

From the front car jumps a younger man, *Fernando*, who rushes to shake our hands. We have never seen him before.

"I have business I must tend to," explains the friendly Julio as he turns to us. "Fernando works for me. He will drive you to Valladolid at our agreed price. However, it is best not to take the cuota (toll) road because it is closed. Fernando will take you via the little towns and you will come safely to Valladolid but it may take a little longer."

After our luggage has been moved to the bona fide taxi, Julio enthusiastically pumps our hands, welcomes us again, addresses Fernando in Spanish and waves goodbye.

We have no choice. Fernando is now our driver. He speaks no English. We speak minimal Spanish. It would be easy for us to suspect something was amiss.

And so, we are off to Valladolid.

When we hit the main highway, we understand what Julio means about the toll road. It is a mess. Torn up so badly that at times the four lanes shrink to two, one lane each for coming and going traffic. All this in preparation for the Maya Train, a government initiative expected to transport multitudes of tourists. On completion this will be a 1,525-kilometre (948 mi) intercity railway in Mexico that will traverse the Yucatán Peninsula with stops along the way at the many Maya archeological ruins.

Despite Julio's instructions to drive through the small towns, Norm directs Fernando to take the toll road. Neither of us relishes the thought of driving through small Yucatecan towns of winding roads liberally sprinkled with *topes* (speed bumps).

It was a good decisión. We arrive at our destination in approximately two hours, as planned.

So, we ask ourselves, did we outfox those high-priced airport taxi-drivers?

Well, it's all about the thrill of finding a great deal. Isn't it?

TOMATOES AND DOGS AND SCORPIONS, OH MY!

We return from this land of tamales and iguanas to our Canadian homeland in a few days. But first, a few postcards from the Yucatán's Valladolid colonial city where we have lived for three months.

Gentleman Vendor

In the people's market, a ten-minute walk away, food stalls line the 'walls' under a temporary tent structure of wooden pallets and tarpaulin. They stretch at least two long Canadian city blocks. We shop here for local fresh fruit and vegetables. Although we only speak Spanglish, we enjoy the verbal exchanges.

The vendors probably find us --- and other visiting gringos --- amusing. Or a huge bother. They watch with much curiosity. What we buy. How we pinch-test the avocados. Or ask the name of a weird looking food that looks like oversized kiwi fruit. (*zapote*, they reply, *muy dulce...very sweet*).

There is one problem with shopping at the market, though. These vendors cannot change large denominations of pesos. Their produce costs small amounts. And often we forget that.

Last week we stopped at the stall of an elderly male vendor --- he with *mucho* wrinkles, small chocolate-coloured eyes, white strands of hair, and a kind face --- who was selling tomatoes. We chose a few, asked how much. Norm handed him more than the agreed amount because he had no small change. The old man looked at the pesos and shook his head. We understood him to say we were paying too much for what we bought. Said he was sorry but couldn't make any change.

No problemo, we said, indicating he should keep the extra money.

This would not do for the old fellow. He looked at his table, picking up one tomato after another. Finally, he chose a larger tomato to make up for our overpayment. Handed it to us with a missing tooth smile.

The tomato was heart-shaped.

Beware the Roof Dogs

Lesson One: when walking in many Latino cities, keep your eyes on the ground otherwise you will break a leg: broken sidewalks, sudden sink holes and dips, mysterious liquids, strewn garbage, low hanging signs on which to hit your head. It's all part of the walking obstacle course.

And then, there are the roof dogs.

In Valladolid, and elsewhere in Mexico, most cement *casas* are flat-roofed. This in case the owner decides to add another floor when there is enough money to do so. Many people use that flat roof as another 'living' room. Some have chairs on the roof. Others have plants. Makes sense to increase your living space when you don't have much.

However, while concentrating on navigating the broken sidewalk, remember these flat roofs are sometimes home to the owners' dogs. Recently, while walking, we heard a low menacing growl. Our instincts snapped to attention. Looking up, we gasped in fear at the sight of open canine jaws: the many-fanged mouth of a drooling roof dog! Ready to pounce on us! This Guard Dog from Hell follows alongside us from atop the roof --- not far from the street --- and snarls and snaps and pants and bares his fangs, threatening to leap and attack us, though he doesn't - an intimidating, terrifying experience.

El Escorpión

One particularly groggy, I mean me --- I was groggy --- morning in Valladolid, I struggled to tell my brain it was time to exercise.

The morning was already hot (24 degrees) and I hadn't slept well because of the heat and well, staying in bed seemed a far better idea than hauling out my exercise mat and attempting half-hearted yoga poses.

In somewhat of a trance, I grabbed my exercise mat to unroll along the tiled floor.

That's when I did a double-take. It looked like a dead leaf --- a curled rusty-coloured vegetation at first glance --- clinging to my exercise mat.

I went to touch it, fling it off, and proceed with my floor exercises. For some reason, I thought to inspect it more closely.

That's when I realized that was no plant hanging on my mat.

"Norm," I clamoured --- not too hysterically --- "I think there's a scorpion on my exercise mat."

He dropped his weights. Hurried over. Confirmed my worst fears. "That's a scorpion," he agreed.

Quickly he picked up my rolled-up exercise mat, rushed to the door, shook the mat until the small but dangerous demon dropped off. Then he stepped on it with one of his running shoes. Dead. We watched for signs of life. Nada.

And then, fascinated, we watched at the sudden arrival of an army of tiny red ants. As if practising military manoeuvres, they surrounded the scorpion body and as one, began moving it into the grass where they could munch on their unexpected delicacy.

No more groggy me. Suddenly I was wide awake.

Scorpions on your exercise mat will do that for you. A jolt of instant adrenaline.

And then… there's Tigré…

We knew we were accepted into this middle-class neighbourhood because of Tigré. So-called because of faint tiger-like stripes lining his black fur coat, Tigré belongs to the family across the street. When we first arrived, he barked lustily and long. At us. And in front of us. We were strangers in his territory. His message was clear: Get Out!

It didn't take long, though, until he realized we fell under his heading of added responsibilities.

Now he lies along the front of our shaded driveway, surveying his neighbourhood from this vantage point. If anyone --- like the garbageman --- approaches our territory, he barks mercilessly. He does not stop barking until he perceives any danger to us has passed. Or we tell him the visitors are okay (like the pizza delivery man).

Our three-month stay here ends shortly. We are going to miss Tigré. I wish he could understand.

How do you say goodbye to a sweet dawg who's captured your heart?

NICARAGUA

SLICE OF LIFE ON A NICARAGUAN BUS

"They hang from the bars like monkeys." A Nicaraguan colleague describes his fellow riders this way as we discuss our exhausting daily 1.5 hour one way trip of about 50 km for two months on a local bus from Granada to the capital city of Managua and return.

Packed like sardines, body parts meshed and mingled with scantily clad strangers: ample breasts pressed on bare shoulders, legs jammed into other legs, feet locked into awkward positions, hips hitting buttocks, arms holding purses the size of suitcases, loaded backpacks, heavy packages, all dangling precariously from owners hanging onto overhead bars--- *if* the bus has bars--- this is about as up close and personal as you can get while the bus lurches, lunges, stops and pushes its battered frame through the oppressive heat and traffic tangle of Managua. Buses, many in need of a complete overhaul, seat about 24-30 people but that number swells to more than double during rush hours.

The 30-34 C heat intensifies the experience. Sweating faces welcome any whiff of stuffy polluted air near an open window. Street vendors yelling *"agua...agua...agua...",* braking cars, squealing tires, babies crying on and off the bus, dogs barking, cell phones chirping, music thumping, an assault on our senses; noise, noise, noise.... The people's bus offers a microcosm of daily life in this big city of Nicaragua.

The *copiloto* (driver's assistant) adds to the chaos. Hanging out the side door, he yells in a melodic incantation, whistles and gestures to the waiting crowds anxious to get to work on time: *Managua! Managua! Managua!* His job is to push more passengers into the bus, down the narrow aisle, bare flesh pressing bare flesh. When he can no longer board the bus himself, he ceases to lure people. *Dale! Dale! Dale*! we think he yells to the driver. Whatever he's saying, he means *Go! Go!*

Go! as he hangs out the door supported by one arm locked onto a vertical bar inside the oven-hot vehicle. That's after he's run alongside the bus, hopping on and off in search of passengers.

Now the *copiloto* must collect the fare (one way: 24 córdobas---about US $1). Somehow he weasels his way through the maze and amazingly, despite their discomfort and burdened arms, riders hold money ready in hand. If the *copiloto* cannot reach his intended, fares are passed hand over hand from the back of the bus to him. Córdoba bills, intertwined among his fingers as if growing there, are counted and if necessary, change returns via the same way, hand over hand.

Riding the people's bus is an eye-opening encounter for these two Canadians volunteers teaching English as a Second Language at a university founded to help educate the poor. As the only foreigners riding the bus among native Nicas for many weeks, we learned more about the local culture and life than had we stayed at one of the few posh hotels near *MetroCentro*, a modern shopping centre in the crowded, poor, fast-moving, dangerous, often heartless city of Managua. Alongside sleek gambling joints sit haphazard boxes of sheet metal with dirt floors, homes of the very poor. Garbage is everywhere.

Managua is like a giant aquarium teeming with all types and sizes of fish, vigilant sharks lying in wait ready to gobble up the small or weak at any minute.

In the city, chic office workers and students---the future of Nicaragua---mingle among crowded market vendors, worn-out grannies whose faces are etched in deep creases from years of toiling in the unforgiving sun under harsh conditions, afraid to smile because of missing front teeth. A visible poster campaign extolling the virtues of equality between man and woman has been lost on the older generation who have suffered too many revolutions, earthquakes and much corruption.

As passengers, we witness everyday life in three-dimensional form. Motorcycle accidents are common and often fatal. Traffic snarls force cyclists to weave in and out of stop-go-stop vehicles. Meanwhile on the bus, our *copiloto* cajoles and guides a National Police officer, gun in holster, to board despite the crush of humanity. A young woman, evidently feeling nauseous (an uncomfortable feeling I experienced more than once), sucks on raw ginger.

A hefty female passenger, wanting to get off at the next stop, hoists herself from her seat by grabbing a male passenger around his waist as an anchor. Facing the opposite direction, his eyebrows shoot up with anticipation at the sight of a woman's arms suddenly around him. A coy smile is on his mouth until he turns and sees the enormity of the middle-aged woman's girth. An older woman, held upright by the crush of people, immediately hooks her cane around the back of an empty seat to claim it. No question. It's hers. Standing squashed, but close to the seated me, a young woman has turned her body inward, held in suspension by the human throng surrounding her. Her long wet thick black hair, recently washed, drips white gobs of conditioner down her back, onto my lap. A market woman carries pungent food wares atop her head. Loud pulsing music from the bus radio adds to the raucous mix of sight, sound, and smell.

Our bus stops in the everlasting traffic. A battered truck idles in front of us, piled high with ripe watermelons. Two riders, facing forward, sit atop the mountain of melons. Our *copiloto*, already hanging out the side door, jumps off the bus. As if engrossed in a thriller movie, all passengers watch him. He reaches the old truck a few feet away, takes hold of its worn back wooden railing, climbs quickly hand over hand to the top. Stepping nimbly over the last wooden bar, he picks up a watermelon, steps back over the rotting railing and scrambles back to the bottom. The watermelon lookouts have seen nothing.

Deftly he re-enters the bus. No Hollywood director could match this drama. We love the diversion. Weary hot passengers hoot and holler their approval as the *copiloto* holds aloft the stolen watermelon treasure. We can almost taste the luscious fruit, water dribbling down thirsty, sweating chins. Despite the discomfort, the heat, the pressing flesh, the stomach-churning exhaust fumes, we see no evidence of petty crime (in fact passengers are extremely honest when paying fares and *copilotos* even run to nearby street stalls for change if necessary). People do not complain and are tolerant, even polite, some offering seats to the elderly or handicapped. Others fall into a deep sleep with bobbing heads.

Copilotos are a breed unto themselves. They guide and urge already-stuffed passengers to move on down the aisle, sometimes take parcels and place them on the dashboard, help customers off and on, and all with a gentle touch. Each has his own captivating personality.

The driver concentrates only on driving. Often he blasts his horn handily attached to a hanging rope dangling on his left. Since it's his job to get his customers to their destination despite traffic, potholes and other obstacles, he scoots down side roads, sneaks along the shoulder or diverts to a collecting lane or pulls a U-turn when he can get away with it, completely ignoring any rules of the road. He and his *copiloto* are a well-oiled team. During our weeks of bus riding we never saw -or expected to see- a female driver or *copiloto.* Each bus prominently displays religious paraphernalia proclaiming in Spanish, *God bless us; Jesus is our Saviour; God rides with us.* Perhaps these slogans explain the foolhardy behaviour.

It is because of our heady bus riding experience we learn how hard Nicas work, long hours in tedious jobs for little pay. Those without a job, or underemployed as many are, eke out a meagre existence with little hope of breaking the poverty cycle. Riding a packed Nicaraguan bus to and from the big city has given us a compelling glimpse of the country's real people: warm, friendly and accommodating despite their tough lives.

Nicaragua Fast Facts

Nicaragua, the poorest country in Central America and the second poorest in the Western Hemisphere (after Haiti), has widespread underemployment and poverty. Almost one out of six Nicaraguans live on less than US$1.25/day. (*Source: CIDA Canadian International Development Agency)*

A BOY IN NICARAGUA HAUNTS ME

He appeared suddenly on my left.

Because we arrived in León, Nicaragua, late last night we were tired so his presence did not register immediately when we left our BnB with glazed eyes. We came to spend three months here to avoid the cold Canadian winter… to experience life in a third world country, the second poorest in the western hemisphere after Haiti…to leave our comfort zone, test ourselves in a foreign land. This was not our first visit to Nicaragua so we already knew about her warm and hospitable people.

In the morning, following a hard travel day and a restless sleep, we had just stepped from our accommodation onto the uneven, narrow sidewalk, turning to our right. Out of thin air, he appeared on my left. A boy about 8 with large brown eyes. He said nothing. But he raised his hand, waving fingers frantically in his mouth. I stopped. Stared. Then he vanished.

Seconds later, my mind processed his gesture. The child was hungry. He was asking for food. In a vain effort at redemption, I looked around for him. He was gone.

Trying to forget his haunting look, I continued on with our plan. Our first task in this culturally-rich university city was to find a permanent address. We hoped to rent a *casa* near *centro* where we could walk to the cathedrals, parks, *mercados* and places frequented by locals. Of course, being North American, we wanted internet, a fully equipped kitchen, a clean, modern bathroom and any other amenities to make our life comfortable.

While we looked, though, I kept thinking, *but what about that little boy? Where does he live?*

As we searched, using BnB guest/host contacts, walking around looking for signs to rent (*alquilar*), frequenting tourist bureaus, visiting real estate offices, scouring the internet, we began to lose hope. Small *casas* we saw were too far away or else bare, dirty and dark shanties, begging for TLC, not in great neighbourhoods.

During this time of reconnaissance, we discovered other facets of life in León. Early mornings in our *Paz de Luna (Peace of the Moon)* BnB, brought squawks from green parrots as flocks visited the inner lush courtyard with its running water fountain and plethora of tropical plants: birds of paradise, aloe, hibiscus, flowering cacti, sour orange trees; in the dining room we lingered over breakfast and the background music of legendary crooners singing old American standards like *How Insensitive*. We listened to street noises: the enchanting clip clop of small horses' hooves pulling old two-wheeled flat wagons along narrow, cobblestone streets. The sounds sent my mind tumbling back to a more seductive past.

Lest I paint too romantic a picture, please be aware of the opposites. We cannot flush tissue down toilets in this city: *Please do not put any paper in the toilet to avoid plumbing problems.* Used tissues must be deposited in the garbage bin located beside the toilet. Although León is relatively clean, watch you don't break a leg on the many sidewalk potholes and chunks of broken pavement. Pockets of poverty---a weary elderly shoeshine man with bent back hoisting his trade tools across the central square; an old, barefoot woman peddling postcards; a younger one, tired already, extending her hand--- exist alongside scores of university students sitting on the cathedral's base scanning their cell phones.

I watch a group of four boys, 8-10 years, jostle along the street with slingshots ready, their eyes on a moving target along the side of a building. The shortest one takes aim on the run, fires, and whoops with joy. The friends run together to the wall where the hunter picks up and proudly displays his fallen prey, a lifeless iguana.

As we retrace the steps to our BnB, I spy a long, lean, and gaunt older gentleman dressed in black, trailing closely behind us. His hair is sparse and grey. His bearing is regal. We enter *Paz de Luna;* he automatically follows. Startled, I turn to investigate before we disappear to our room. I see him approach the desk, motioning in his mouth with waving fingers. This time I signal to the female staff, *we will pay for his food.* She smiles, nods, shows him to a table.

The frail stranger, sitting with back straight, is staring out the window at the clear, cloudless day, waiting patiently for food. He does not see us.

That's when I recall the painted message on the wall of a local café, *Pan y Paz* (Bread and Peace)… *the world would be a better place if everyone had bread and peace everyday.*

Which reminds me again of the street boy with the brown eyes. I saw him for only a second but he will haunt me for a lifetime.

The Bug on the Bus and Tarantula in the Drawer

Ever wonder what becomes of those ugly yellow Bluebird school buses when they're almost junk? They start a new life in Central America.

The bus I'm on now is in León, Nicaragua. I'm squished into a torn, well-worn window seat on this over crowded hot bus, next to the non-functioning sliding window.

Inhaling my foreign surroundings, I spy an ominous looking bug, just out of reach, watching me from the side panel under the window. The bug is actually closer to the bare arms of the pony-tailed young woman in the seat ahead of me. She is engaged in a lively conversation otherwise I would warn her --- despite my limited Spanish skills --- about the nasty looking bug.

This insect, carrying a black hard shell with red wavy lines, is about the size of my thumbnail. Its antennae are long and waving. Somehow resting comfortably on the side panel of the bus, it faces me. Right now, the bug is stationary. And I am caught in its line of vision.

There is too much activity and noise on this bus…and we haven't left the depot yet.

A large middle-aged woman from the market is pushing along the crowded aisle hawking *tajadas,* a favourite Nica snack of fried plantains served in a plastic bag with two helpings of coleslaw salad (carried separately in a swinging pail) topped with a splash of some mysterious sauce. The woman's eye makeup is impeccable but over the top: turquoise eyelids with a whitish blend beneath her carefully black pencilled eyebrows. Shimmering tomato red lips draw attention to her double chins. The colour of her lips matches her long fake fingernails. Tawny coloured hair, black at the roots, is pulled back severely into a pony-tail accenting her dangling golden hoop earrings. She is a study in extremes as she sways back and forth, up and down the crowded aisle, hawking her food.

Her loud appearance is a magnet, forcing me to take my eye off the bug for a minute. But suddenly my peripheral vision senses movement. I catch the bug's slow silent creep towards me along the side panel of this hot-like-a-furnace vehicle.

Finally, the aging bus burps and smokes as the driver pulls out onto the dusty road. He switches an old Bruce Lee film on the front video screen which adds to the general confusion.

Nica buses have a *copiloto,* a helper who performs duties that free the driver to do his job. The *copiloto* collects fares, helps passengers off and on the bus, urges them to move on back when it's crowded. Our *copiloto* is slowly making his way through the stand of pressed-together flesh, collecting the fare, while the bus is in motion.

The bug, still there and visible in my peripheral vision, unsettles me. I decide to flick it away but miss my flick; instead, it skitters closer to the bare arm of the girl ahead of me. Unfortunately, it still faces me, ignoring the luscious looking flesh only one bite away.

Now careening along the highway with swaying customers leaning into and around our bus seats, I decide it's time to warn the pony-tailed girl about the bug. As I'm about to tap her shoulder, she pulls a canister from her large purse, sprays her thick black hair and unwittingly sprays the ominous looking bug. It disappears --- where? On my bare leg? Inside my shorts? In my backpack wedged into the space between my legs, ready to pop out when least suspected?

Meanwhile, back at our casa

The bug is still on my mind when we awaken the next morning to the crow of nearby roosters. Too many *insectos* in these tropical countries, I conclude.

Suddenly my husband beckons me to the *baño*.

"Spider," he whispers, "big one." He points to an open drawer.

I gasp.

Tarantula! Two of its black hairy legs hang over the edge, poised as if ready to jump.

Oh, what to do? What to do? Although a whiz at defeating bugs, my husband has no idea how to tackle a 10 cm tarantula.

Is it fast? Poisonous? Aggressive? We run around in circles before he decides to seek an expert: he runs for help from a Nica neighbour. *Ayúdame! Help me!* I hear him shout.

While he's gone only a minute, I nervously eye the tarantula in case the creature decides to scurry somewhere. Like towards ME.

My husband returns *pronto* with our aging Nica neighbour. He sees the tarantula. No translation necessary.

Reaching into his back pocket, he whips out one of those spring-loaded tape measures that when released flies back inside its canister. While we both watch intently, our elderly neighbour pulls out the tape measure to a desired length.

Deftly, quickly, he places the extended tape under the body of the tarantula, immediately flips it out of the drawer, onto the floor. Stunned, the huge spider does not move. With lightning speed, our saviour neighbour steps on it.

There, before our astonished eyes, we stare open-mouthed at the remains of this large hairy intruder. Squished into many black hairy pieces.

Immediately I think about all the dark places in our rented *casa* where his kin might hide. Undisturbed black corners of our bedroom closet. Hidden back-of-the-drawer spaces, like cupboards. Behind the stove. Even under the bed at night.

And to think I was worried about the bug on the bus.

The Old Man by the Church

Is he homeless? Sick? What is he doing here? How did he get here? Where is he from?

A one-legged amputee, the old man sits on the ground leaning beside his wheelchair and against the black wrought iron fence that borders the church in our neighbourhood of Zaragoza. One day he is not there, the next day he is.

We regularly walk seven blocks to *centro* for shopping, banking, park concerts in León, Nicaragua, where we are living for three months; the Zaragoza Church is enroute. So the old man's appearance is sudden and surprising. During our first pass, I glance surreptitiously at him. A small bundle of belongings is heaped on the seat of his wheelchair. Loose plastic grocery bags containing mysterious items are scattered around him. It is morning, no shade on this side of the church. He wears no hat although the sun beats mercilessly down on him. Coupled with 30 C (90 F) plus degree temperatures, he has to feel uncomfortable even if he is Nicaraguan. As a visitor I know I suffer from the heat, sweating profusely while seated on a bench in the shade.

Surely, we think when we first see him, the good people of the church will help him. Maybe that's why he's chosen this spot to rest his tired and crippled body.

But no. We are alarmed he is still there the next day, and the next day, and the next….each time we pass, he is there. We also notice scraps of food around him. We deduce people feed him, including us. Each time we return from grocery shopping at the *supermercado*, we drop something off at his feet if he is dozing or in his lap if he is awake.

First, it is a *mandarino*, then a boxed fruit drink, and soon a small snack of fruit, chicken pastry, and a drink. Initially he says nothing, eyes constantly closed as if waiting for death. Later he appears more alert and we hear *gracias*, once I heard 'thank you'.

Six weeks later and the old man is still here. His sidewalk space outside the church is expanding. Someone has dropped off a large cardboard box, perhaps for shelter from the sun. Numerous pieces of food lie sprinkled around him. His position is the same since he parked himself there.

We figure someone must look after his personal needs. Although my husband says he smells a strong odour of urine in his vicinity, we note the old man's gray hair and matching beard is cut and groomed. His face is weathered, sun damaged.

Many weeks later, as we amble along our usual route to *centro*, we notice a blue pick-up truck parked at the curb beside the old man. Two strong-looking men are standing in the back of the truck, having a discussion. Their body language speaks of hesitancy: one has his elbow bent, arm crooked, hand resting on the side of his face, a pose of reflection. We alter our route, turn right instead of heading straight, decide not to pass by the church this time.

Earlier we had asked about the old man with a neighbouring Nicaraguan, a friend fluent in English. He says there are many people like the old man. He says authorities want to place these people somewhere else, out of the line of vision of visitors. City fathers do not want tourists to see the visible poor who lie prostrate in door wells, unfortunates wasted by illegal drugs, civil war cast-offs from decades ago still suffering post traumatic stress disorders. These ugly sights are not for the tourist who comes to Nicaragua for a good time: sun, sea, volcano boarding, eco cloud forest trekking, all for much cheaper rates than neighbouring Costa Rica.

I think of home and the destitute people I see in downtown Toronto, seeking shelter from the cold winter winds, lying on flattened cardboard pieces placed over sidewalk grates to catch whiffs of heat from subway lines racing below the streets. Or indigenous people whose communities lack clean water and a clean environment, where young people see suicide as the only way out. Canada is a first world country; Nicaragua is third world.

On our return to our *casa* from the *supermercado*, prepared to drop off his usual fare, we discover the old man's wheelchair has disappeared; the sidewalk is clean, no sign of habitation or garbage. No odours. Out of sight, out of mind.

An unwanted liability, the old man is gone.

ECUADOR

ECO ETIQUETE ON THE ENCHANTED ISLANDS

"Watch where you're stepping!"

I flinch. Our naturalist guide, Nikolas, is talking to me. Excited by being mere inches from the stuffed toy-like sea lions on Española Island, one of many in the Galápagos archipelago in the Pacific Ocean off the coast of Ecuador, and eager for a close-up portrait, I have committed a cardinal sin by straying from the marked path.

"See these rock boundaries?" repeats Nikolas. "They are there so you know where you can walk and where you can't. If you wander over you can do so much damage. Without knowing it, you can step on iguana egg nests buried in the sand or a bird's ground nest. So just remember---please---stay on the path."

Unfortunately, I stumble again into the pit of ignorance although this time I am not alone.

"Puh-leeze!" pleads Nikolas to everyone. "No flashes on the camera! This is not good for the animals. And please do not touch them. They have no fear of humans since we do not harm them." A sea lion pup, nursing with his mom, looks up with big warm brown eyes, and then nonchalantly turns back to his milk supply. We are enchanted. No wonder these are called The Enchanted Islands.

Slowly but surely I am learning the proper rules of etiquette in The Galápagos National Park and Marine Reserve as we carefully wind our way along narrow trails, some of them treacherous and slippery from water and shards of hard lava.

We move on and quietly observe a mama, papa and baby blue-footed booby family, the chick a mass of ruffled soft feathers.

The bird's bright blue feet, coloured as if a child has used a paint-by-number set, are used in a mating ritual in which the adults lift up their feet and dance around, sometimes pointing their wings towards the sky.

"You see," whispers Nikolas. "You might have stepped on their nests if you wandered off the trail." We get the message as we watch the fascinating family at our feet.

On we tread---carefully. We come across a pair of mating marine iguanas, the red and green male ("we call them Christmas iguanas", says Nikolas) atop the squirming red and black female. Again, we are only a few feet away.

Suddenly, to Nikolas's delight, he spies a 'waved albatross'. "This is something," he exclaims. "I thought they had all left the island but this one is young and still a bit heavy."

The waved albatross must actually take off like an airplane over the island cliffs depending entirely on the southeast trade winds to carry him to feeding areas. We watch the bird run back and forth repeatedly in a practice session. Soon he will shed enough weight as he matures and be able to lift off.

Sally Lightfoot crabs (named by English seafarers) scamper over a black volcanic landscape like bright orange plastic toys, their multi-coloured markings a work of art.

So much to share about life on these enchanted islands! Perhaps this appetizer will entice you to visit and experience the abundant wild and marine life there. It is a humbling and powerful education into Mother Nature's extraordinary survival processes.

Rules of the National Park:

PLEASE!

- stay on the trails
- do not disturb any wildlife or remove any native plant or rock material

- make sure you do not accidentally transport any live material to the islands, or from island to island. Insular ecosystems are fragile biological units.

- be cautious when approaching wildlife and always follow your Naturalist's advice.

- animals are not to be fed by humans.

- it is prohibited to bring food to visitor sites

- do not startle or chase any animal from its resting or nesting area

- smoking is not allowed on the islands nor is it in any boat during your visits. The use of cellular phones is prohibited on visitor sites

- do not buy any souvenirs made from native Galápagos species (exception: wood)

The Galápagos Islands

The islands are a group of 13 major volcanic islands that lie in the Pacific about 600 miles (1,000 km) off the coast of Ecuador. 97% comprise the National Park and Marine Reserve.

It is the world's largest marine reserve after the Great Barrier Reef of Australia. The islands are relatively new geologically, ranging in age from 4-5 million years to just less than one million years old. There is continuous geologic activity as the islands evolve. The equator bisects the Galápagos.

Charles Darwin visited the islands in 1835 for five weeks. He noticed striking differences between the wildlife and plants here compared with the mainland. These observations formed the beginning of his thoughts about evolution.

Evolutionary processes are found in species such as the 13 Darwin finches (believed to be descendants of a common ancestor), Galápagos mockingbirds, giant tortoises, flightless cormorants (so named because they have no need to fly due to a plentiful food supply and lack of predators),

Galápagos penguins (third smallest in the world and the only ones in the northern hemisphere) plus certain cacti and the Scalesia tree (from the aster family). 40% of the 500 higher plant species are endemic to the islands. Out of more than 400 species of fish found in and around the islands, 50 are endemic. Of the 58 species of birds found here, 28 are endemic.

The most famous reptiles of the islands are the giant tortoises with 14 subspecies, of which three are extinct. The Pacific green sea turtle is the only marine turtle endemic to the Galápagos. Another endemic reptilian species are the iguanas. The marine iguana, the Santa Fe land iguana and the Galápagos land iguana are all endemic to the area.

PANAMA

WHEN THE GOING GETS TOUGH, THE TOUGH GET GOING

High country in Panama means tough work for me. Not so for husband Norm.

While wintering in this Central American country--- known mostly for its famous canal--we decided to overnight at an inland Eco Lodge, **Los Quetzales,** a far cry from the Panama Canal, and hike 1975 metres high in the mountains near the Costa Rican border,. We needed good weather for a planned early morning start on the guided hike at a higher elevation. Clouds, rain, and mist are the norm in this area. Sunshine is a coveted bonus so the night before our trek, as we sipped our manhattans ---instead of healthy smoothies--- in front of a roaring lounge fire, we prayed for favour from the sun gods.

My first setback was lack of sleep. While Norm falls instantly asleep after an organic filet mignon meal with copious amounts of fine *vino*, I lie like a board in the darkness, unable to relax. Different sounds surround me: insects, nocturnal grunts and groans, creaking boards, strange unidentifiable noises. Worse, I ate too much at dinner and feel like a humungous porpoise lying in thin air, breathing with difficulty. Willing sleep so I could awaken refreshed was impossible. The more I demanded my body to relax, the more it rebelled.

The morning (ah so, I must have fallen asleep) dawned bright and beautiful with the sound of chirping exotic birds. The sun god must have heard our prayers. No need for raingear or fears of sloshing around in mountain mud. At breakfast, I am not hungry so nibble on hard-boiled eggs and excellent Panamanian coffee (to keep me alert).

We meet our guide, Abel---pronounced Ah-bell---who speaks only Spanish with a smattering of English (we speak English with a smattering of Spanish). He says he'll drive us to the trail entrance as it's farther up the mountain. He's driving a tractor trailer as the 'road' is impossible to navigate with any other vehicle. We sit bumping along in the trailer behind his diesel-spewing tractor. Finally, he stops at a wooden shack where we must change to rubber boots. Many pairs of rubber boots are lined up for eager hikers. "You need," he advises.

This tractor trailer ride over the rock-and-mud lane is so jagged and ragged and diesel-smelling, I am nauseated. Mercifully, before my stomach empties, we arrive at *Parque Amistad* (Friendship Park), a joint park with Costa Rica that includes cloud forests in both countries. Annually there is 5,000 mm. of rain with an average temperature range from 8 – 14 degrees C (46 – 57 F). Lucky for us, it is a pleasant 18 C (65 F). Lucky we are wearing boots and lucky, too, the sun still shines.

We hike the Three Waterfalls Trail (*Sendero Tres Cascadas*) rated **moderate difficult**. Before we commit, Abel looks me over as if judging cattle, nods, and decides I can do it. Norm, fit and eager, is a given. Our primary goal is to sight a *quetzal*, after which the lodge is named. The *quetzal,* a beautiful and colourful long-feathered bird native to Central American cloud forests is the national symbol of Guatamala where their currency is also called the *quetzal.* While bumping along the mountain trek earlier, we discussed and dismissed the likelihood we would see this grand bird. We thought we'd be in the cloud forest shortly after dawn when birds are active. After our long haul up the mountain it is now close to 10 a.m.

The degree of hiking difficulty is equal to the challenging terrain. Up, up, up about 200-300m (650 – 985 ft) to a peak at 2,269m (7444 ft). Then down, down, down to a stream which we forded several times. The estimated time for the 1km (0.62mi) was 90 min. We took two hours due to many stops for photos and to see and hear birds. What is not recorded in these stats are my legs. Many times during the ascent, Norm had to reach down and hoist me up. Thigh muscles burned. Breathing laboured. Arms pulled out of sockets. Sweat on my forehead in the cool air. When I dared glance up, I saw only an everlasting trail. Finally, at the summit, with a glorious view and a fearful inner voice crying *how the hell are we getting down?* Abel calls a halt. He knows I need a break because he hears me huff and puff. While relaxing on an ant-infested log, he calmly confirms that yes, there are jaguars in the vicinity. He proceeds with the story of three hiking gringos *without a guide* he notes, who decided to trek across the peaks along a less travelled trail. When they failed to reach their destination, a search party was launched. The only traces found were a shoe and a ripped backpack. I gulp and look around at the dancing shadows in this remote cloud forest. Abel offers us a local berry he has picked nearby that tastes like lychee fruit. They do not sit well on my stomach. Then we are off again.

"Now," he says looking directly at me, certain I will be happy, "we go down."

So why am I not relieved? Ever trek down a narrow trail with hidden traps like gnarled tree roots, muddy embankments, deep chasms, sudden branches, snapping wood, entwining vines, protruding rocks, possible unfriendly critters and insects? Especially when your thighs are already screaming? Once again Norm proves his chivalry and helps me navigate the lo-o-o-ng trip down to the bottom stream.

By the time we reach the rushing waters of the cold mountain waters with its waterfalls (over which we forded many times), I am physically exhausted.

Yet, like a masochist, I am pleased we trekked this trail. I am pleased my aching arms and legs held out. I am especially pleased we returned safely. I am woman. I am strong.

COLOMBIA

DRINKING DRAGON'S BLOOD

Parque Arví spreads across one of Medellin's mountain saddles. The city of Medellin is surrounded by the Andes Mountains at 1524 m (5,000 ft) above sea level.

So, it is understandable that Arvi was essentially forgotten for about 450 years. And with the ensuing and overwhelming urbanization of the area, it is amazing this unique park did not fall victim to permanent damage.

Thanks to some bureaucratic foresight, almost unheard of in many cases, there are now five parks located within Parque Arví.

Rediscovered

Arví is named for the Indigenous people who once inhabited the region. This was an area which had partially become deforested over the years due to the use of its trees for firewood and lumber by the local population. A familiar occurrence everywhere in the world.

Restored

Fortunately, however, the local utility company purchased 2400 hectares (5900 acres) in the 1940s with the agreement from provincial and Medellin governments to reforest necessary areas.

Reforestation exploded with fast growing trees (such as eucalyptus, pine and cypress) from Canada, US, Mexico, China, Australia and Brazil. Currently, the forest does contain a mix of Colombian trees and plants.

And today the park is home to over 70 species of birds, 72 species of butterflies, 19 species of mammals, and many unique flowers, including several species of orchids.

Parque Arví is unique in size and location. It sits at an elevation of about 2500m (8200ft), 1000m above Medellin.

Getting there and getting oriented

For us, located in the neighbourhood of Poblado in Medellin, it took about 1 ½ hours to reach the park. We hopped a bus, rode the Metro and two cable car lines to get there - about 1 1/2 hours.

Once there, after a swaying cable car ride that overlooks some of the ghetto barrios of Medellin, we jumped off into another greener, safer, world. The park features sections of pre-Hispanic construction, including antique buildings, water works, platforms, roads, gardens and ditches.

We also walked with the ancients: a stone trail featuring some well-preserved sections. Called "Camino Cieza de León" or the "Pre-Hispanic Trail", believed to be more than 1500 years old.

Intrigue leads to the Dragon's Blood

Most trails are low-difficulty. Experienced guides (some English speaking) stand ready at the entrance to lead you on fascinating discoveries. Of twelve popular trails, three hint of intrigue: Ancestral, Bewitched, Myths and Legends.

Gustavo, our guide, points out a heart-shaped leaf from a tree explaining it is known locally as "Arbol de Drago", the dragon tree (*croton lechieri*). "The sap from this tree is red like blood," he says. From which comes the name 'dragon's blood'.

The leaf of the dragon tree is incorporated into the park's insignia.

Gustavo explains the medicinal properties of Dragon's Blood/ Sangre de Drago are well-known among the Indigenous people of South America.

Locals use the dark red sap to help alleviate or heal a wide variety of ailments. It is reputed to boost the immune system as well as promote the healing of gastrointestinal problems like ulcers, diarrhea, nausea and vomiting.

Dragon's Blood: almost the perfect medicine?

The sap is also reportedly a diuretic. It prevents dandruff, can be used on the skin to ease acne and insect bites and a few drops will form a protective coat on a cut, like a liquid bandage, to stop bleeding.

Health Benefits for all

The list of health benefits attributed to Dragon's Blood, *Sangre de Drago*, is long: it even helps fight against memory loss, intestinal parasites, sore throats, and hemorrhoids.

Indigenous women apparently use a solution of it to wash out the vagina before childbirth.

Cure-all

There are bolder claims Dragon's Blood is beneficial in the fight against cancer, tuberculosis, erectile dysfunction and more...it seems a few absorbed drops of this liquid is a cure-all!

Perhaps there are still miracles of medicine to discover in the natural world.

Internet

Internet research indicates there have been some U.S. patents registered to study the anti-viral and healing properties of Dragon's Blood.

And a quick search also reveals the dark viscous liquid is sold on the internet.

But did we sample Dragon's Blood?

Not surprisingly after our educational hike in Arvi, we headed directly to a natural health store in Medellin and asked for Dragon's Blood. The proprietor fetched a small plastic container of purified Sangre de Drago with no additives at a cost of about $2 USD (maybe more now). Recommended daily dosage is 3 – 5 drops in a quarter cup of water for maximum health benefits.

So, did we actually use Sangre de Drago?

Well, ask our friends. They wonder why we're breathing fire.

CANADA

LAND OF GHOSTS AND MOUNTAINS

Haunted Saloon

Half the fun of finding the Last Chance Saloon in the haunted *Rosedeer Hotel* in Wayne (blink your eyes and it's gone), Alberta, is meandering along a narrow valley dusty road beside the Rosebud River.

Locals call this the Eleven Bridges Road; all eleven are short, wood planked, and one lane. The Guinness Book of Records lists this unique road as having the most bridges in the shortest distance.

On our summer motor trip to Canada's west, the antiquated Rosedeer Hotel was not on our agenda. Then a local guide whispered:...*Rosedeer. Haunted. 'Tween bridges 9 and 10. Murder. Last Chance Saloon, best buffalo burgers ....12.8km* southeast of Drumheller.

The Last Chance Saloon in the Rosedeer Hotel, over 100 years old, is a slice of the old Wild West. It is the background star in movies like *Running Brave*, Truman Capote's *In Cold Blood*, and Jackie Chan's *Shanghai Noon*. Wayne, the village in which it is located, once boasted 3,000 inhabitants; 2,000 were miners. Today's town sign reads population, 33.

Before the Eleven Bridges Road, everything and everyone to do with the once active Rosedeer Coal Mine across from the Rosedeer Hotel, came in by railroad.

'Twas one wild and lawless town. Mine workers favoured the Communist Party and in the 1920s Ku Klux Klan members lit crosses on the hills. A previous hotel owner said at that time the Last Chance bar was known as the Bucket of Blood because of miners' fights. When coal mining was in full swing some Ukrainian and Russian miners wanted to form a union. The company brought in several KKK union busters. They beat up a number of union organizers, two of whom died in a room on the third floor. This ended the call for unionization but created a haunted room still available for rent.

Bullet holes in the saloon's wall are framed above the piano, testimony to the time in 1970 when three strangers walked into the Last Chance, ordered drinks and refused to pay. The bartender calmly walked back to the bar, pulled out a 45-calibre revolver and shot three bullets, each one over the heads of the defiant customers who soon fled the scene. Bar walls are crammed with memorabilia with old-time memorabilia.

There are no other businesses in Wayne. There used to be a post office, store and a few others but only the hotel remains, although young people are now attracted by the village's unique reputation.

We thought about staying the night in the haunted room. That was before the current owner showed us a couple of photos on his cell phone of ghostly images taken by a patron a few weeks ago and forwarded to him. For sure we see two ethereal outlines leaning forward just behind the bar.

As we sip bourbons and munch on buffalo burgers, the female bartender shares her paranormal story. While working the bar, she heard someone call her name several times. Despite her search, she never located the caller. Some of her bar help also mentioned they heard her voice calling them---and she wasn't on-site. Each chalked it up to another visit by ghosts of the past.

WINTER WONDERLAND

I am caught. Sinking into deep snow, my husband finally pulls me from a leg lock. I cannot see. My vision is reduced by swirls of thick, spinning snowflakes in this wild world of white.

But....this is fun!

We are in the midst of a whiteout in an elevated area around Smithers, northern British Columbia, Canada. Hudson Bay Mountain---height: 1650 m/5413 ft---towers above the town giving its alpine designed Main Street the look of a Swiss Alps village.

Until I see it again through the eyes of children, I forgot about the magic of winter.

Who has ever tasted and shared the warmth and camaraderie of hot spiced rum atop a craggy peak after a long climb in deep snow? We have. In Smithers. The trek was part of an annual neighbourly tradition during which smudging with smouldering sage detoxified our souls and squares of dark chocolate lingered decadently on our tongues. Most important task? Flying strings of Tibetan prayer flags, unfurled and attached to nearby tree trunks. Each triangular piece of coloured cloth flapped in the wind carrying silent meditations towards heaven.

Then came the fun part for children. Slogging further up the mountain we stood in awe, gazing at the surrounding snow-clad mountain tops. Kids tobogganed and slid down the long steep slope. Finally snowed out, they carefully zig-zagged to the bottom. Tired, wet and hungry, like horses making for the barn, they led their toboggans along a rough path, down to the snow-covered road and waiting home alive with twinkling lights, warm hearth, and hearty food and drink liberally sprinkled with friends and laughter.

Swirling snow almost obliterated the trails for horse-drawn old-fashioned sleighrides. Two magnificent 1000 pound draft horses, the Percherons of French origin, pulled each large and loaded sled. Kids took over the first sleigh; adults and toddlers reserved the second one---the latter arrangement removed any danger of errant snowballs or loose, icy branches flung with abandon. Suddenly, what to our wondering eyes should appear? But a snowsuit clad adult carrying a flask of whiskey which he generously shared among us.

With jingling bells, the mighty Percherons pulled their human cargo up, down, and around thick woods until a half way stop: a crackling bonfire around which to thaw frozen fingers and toes, roast hot dogs and marshmallows, and sip hot chocolate.

Living in northern B.C., you must downhill/cross country ski or snowboard, otherwise miss out on more fun and exercise. The Bulkley Valley Nordic Centre, perched amidst a spruce forest on the way to Hudson Bay Mountain, offers 45 km of trails for cross country skiers.

Farther up the road, the popular HBM Resort demands you challenge its awesome slopes of powder snow....36 runs, 4 lifts, a base depth of 86 cm....you can even ski off the mountain on a special Trail to Town that leads you all the way down to Smithers below!

On the day we visited the ski hill, a cloud cover kept the valley shrouded in a continuous dull fog. As we drove up, up, nearing the ski resort, the car suddenly broke through the thick screen and we were above the clouds in another land. A bright blue sky and strong sun greeted us along with jubilant skiers. As high as we were, it was still impossible to see Bulkley Valley below because of its misty barrier.

Of course, winter isn't winter without gliding across the ice on blades or shooting a hockey puck in a net. Skating in a frigid zone (minus 15 degrees C) on an outside rink under a canopy of twinkling stars with a full moon showering dazzling diamonds across the snow provided the perfect combination of a Canadian winter. My husband looked as smooth on the ice as he did during his university hockey days.

While local black bears hibernate and moose wander the land in search of food, Smithers thrives under the cloak of Old Man Winter.

BEAR COUNTRY

"No. No bear sightings for at least 3 weeks." "Naw, haven't seen nary a one for a few weeks now." "Too late in the season. Ya won't see bears now."

The desk clerk, game warden, park ranger: all agree the bears have moved on.

With two young grandsons, we drove north to Stewart, BC/Hyder, Alaska, planning to watch grizzly and/or black bears chow down on salmon as the adult fish fight their way upstream to spawn and die. We hope to see one of these magnificent animals from the bear viewing platform built for this purpose in Hyder.

But then I read safety measures on what to do if in contact with bears and was left with the distinct impression it's best not to meet one! Especially with vulnerable boys, ages 8 to 10.

Here's the advice for a black bear encounter: *If the attack escalates and a black bear physically contacts you, fight back with anything available to you. Black bears tend to be more timid than grizzlies and fighting back may scare off the bear. If a bear is stalking you, then you are in a predatory situation and fighting back is your only option. This also applies to any attack at night...."*

Gulp.

Advice when encountering a grizzly is less comforting: *If you believe the bear is stalking you, fight back with everything you have....Playing dead in a daytime grizzly encounter tends to reduce the level of injury sustained by most attack victims. Many grizzly attacks are defensive in nature and playing dead may show the bear you are not a threat. Keep your backpack on as it provides added protection. Best position is to lie on your side in the fetal position. Bring your legs up to your chest and bury your head into your legs. Wrap your arms around your legs and hold on tight. Do not play dead until the last moment. Staying on your feet may allow you to dodge an attack.*

Double gulp. So I'm actually relieved no-one has seen a bear for a few weeks.

This area we are now in: Stewart BC/Hyder, Alaska, is an odd border landmark. Hyder, population 87, is Alaska's easternmost town, a tiny community surrounded by lofty, glacier-covered peaks at the corner of the Alaska Panhandle, according to Condé Nast Traveler magazine. The town boomed in the early 20th century with the nearby discovery of gold and silver but is now so small residents call it "Alaska's friendliest ghost town." The bear viewing platform lies a few km out of town.

Just ten minutes away is neighbouring Stewart, B.C., our destination for the night. It feels weird to cross an unarmed, unmanned U.S. border, as we did, from Canada to the U.S. On the return trip we---like all travellers---must report to Canadian Customs and Immigration. When we inquire as to why no 'official' U.S. border patrol, the reply is: "there's no place to go after Hyder....only mountains."

The town of Stewart, B.C., is also surrounded by stunning glacial terrain. In early 1898, the lure of gold brought prospectors and miners to the area. By 1918, Stewart was home to a thriving mining community of 10,000. Population today is about 500 scattered among the remains of century old homes, buildings, gravel roads, and historic relics.

In this outpost, often cut off from civilization in the winter due to avalanche activity, we bed down in 20th century accommodation at Ripley Creek Inn, feeling like pioneers of the wild northwest.

But what about the bears?

Well, we cross the unmanned US border into Hyder, Alaska, and find the bear viewing platform overlooking a shallow section of the crystal clear Fish River. A few dozen spectators, some there all day, are patiently waiting for a bear sighting. They all shake their heads when we ask, "any bears?" Our two young fellas watch schools of salmon struggling upstream for awhile and then are bored. We decide it's time to leave.

Suddenly a woman visitor points, whispers excitedly, "BEAR!"

Sure enough, an adult black bear ambles out of the bush across from the viewing platform in full view of onlookers and into the river. He gingerly places his paw in the cool running river as scores of jumping salmon surround him. With a quick swat, he grabs one, splashes back to shore, tears at the fish, stuffing flesh into his mouth.

Wide eyes. Silence. Cameras click. Bear's only focus is salmon. Twice more, under watchful eyes, he wanders into the water to swipe another salmon meal.

We are in awe. Delighted. Privileged. Humbled.

Thank you, Mother Nature, for this special magical experience.

GUIDES OF ROCK AND STONE

One of the best side effects travelling in your own country is the rediscovery of its beauty and the renewed awe one feels about it.

For example, I discovered a phenomenon I didn't know about during our semi-cross country auto voyage from Ontario to British Columbia. I was surprised to see how travellers erected Inukshuks--- stand-alone rock formations in the shape of humans--- at regular intervals along the Canadian Shield sections of the TransCanada Highway in northern Ontario to the Manitoba border.

Inukshuks are stone guides first built by the Inuit years ago to show the way. Today these rock formations symbolize the sense of a caring community; they are friendly reminders that humans have left this monument to point you in the right direction of your journey.

The number of mini Inukshuks astonished me. They are everywhere. Each small statue has its distinct personality, each a reminder of our caring spirit. What fascinated me with these smaller versions were the variations of the rudimentary human form. Different rock colours, sizes, and designs are as original as any piece of sculpture displayed in a contemporary art gallery. Hats off to those travellers who took the time to stop and create their Inukshuks for me to enjoy!

In addition, I learned the word *inukshuk* was recently added to the Oxford English Dictionary. Called a 'loanword' by linguists, inukshuk, borrowed from the Inuktitut language, is defined as 'a structure of rough stones stacked in the form of a human figure'. They are especially prevalent where dynamite is used to blast through the rock for roadbuilding.

Inukshuks were not my only discovery along the northern Ontario route. I used to think Newfoundland was the only Canadian province with picturesque place names. Not. Our northwesterly route took us by Pancake Bay, Pumpkin Point, Rabbit Blanket Lake, Old Woman Bay, Bear Paw Landing. We even followed a dead-end trail in Nipigon to Paddle-to-the-Sea Park.

First Nations names like Shawanaga and Magnetawan dot the landscape, too, conjuring up our colourful history while also dipping me in shame as I think of the plight of First Nations people today.

WHO KNEW ABOUT HOODOOS…?
AND OTHER STRANGE SCENES WILD ROSE COUNTRY

So what's this about hoodoos? Do hoodoos have anything to do with voodoo? Yep.

Hoodoos are fascinating geological formations in the Canadian Badlands . But… what and where are the Canadian Badlands?

Outside Drumheller, Alberta, large hoodoos pierce the sky like sleeping titans in this land French Canadian trappers called *Des mauvaises terrains à traverser*---" badlands to cross".

Reaching towards the sky, hoodoo formations capture the imagination. Origin of their neat name in North America comes from the black magic practices of African Americans in the southern United States (hoodoos are found around the world). With their unusual shapes, their striations of rock and sand in different colours, they look magical. Aboriginals believed they were giants turned to stone for their evil deeds and were harbingers of bad luck .

Standing before hoodoos in the hot sun under a cloudless blue sky, it's easy to understand their attraction. They are cool dudes, or, as they are known in France, 'ladies with hairdos'. Hoodoos are actually formed over thousands of years by erosion. Their solid mushroom-like caps protect the soft, underlying shape.

Drumheller---also known as dinosaur country--- is a fascinating destination. Cute dinosaur replicas with friendly faces dot the townscape leading to the world's largest…a giant 86 foot high Tyrannaurus Rex welcoming you to the visitor centre. I know every tourist destination talks about the longest, highest, best…..well, this is purported to be the world's largest dinosaur statue.

Not far out of town explore and discover more about these extinct creatures at the *world* (another superlative) famous Tyrell Museum. We thought we'd zip through this building (sometimes we get 'museum-ed out') but this is one place where we wish time could stand still. Floor exhibits are educational and well laid out. No boring stuff here.

Still more exciting, wild west drama awaits in the great outdoors not far away, along the Red Deer River valley. Horsethief Canyon conjures up visions of bad guys corralling and herding stolen horses ---after rebranding them for resale--- down the canyon to the U.S. Close your eyes, smell the heat of the day, breathe in the dust of the dry earth ---and you are back in cowboy country.

We cross the Red Deer on a pulley ferry at a narrow section of the river where we bump into the owner guides of a local adventure tour company. While the ferry captain tells us we just missed Brad Pitt (damn!) in a highspeed boat heading upstream with Tom Hanks to check out locales for their latest film on explorers Lewis and Clarke, the seasoned tour operators nod in agreement, explaining this landscape attracts plenty of film makers. Among them, Clint Eastwood who used the locale for some scenes in The Unforgiven.

Tour operators Don and Val also share with us a sometimes overlooked hot spot: site of the Canadian Badlands Passion Play held during July weekends.

Since our visit did not correspond with a live production, Don and Val---in typical western hospitality fashion---invited us to follow their van to the location. What a setting for the passion play! More than 3,000 spectators from around the world view this production during nine sold-out performances each July when it is rain-free. Don challenges us to use our imaginations. He says during a performance actors stand on rock outcroppings surrounding the main stage and in the dark, they add an ethereal dimension to the drama.

Like each Canadian province, Alberta offers a wealth of activity, natural and man-made. And because the wild rose is found across Canada, we wondered how it emerged as Alberta's provincial flower emblem in 1930. At the time, the editor of an Edmonton newspaper suggested the province should select a provincial floral emblem. Eventually Alberta's schoolchildren made the final choice.

TALE OF THE GREEN IGUANA

Once upon a time, an emerald green iguana came to live at our suburban home. His name was Drako and he became the source of local folklore.

One day two salesmen sauntered up the walk to our front door. It was a bubbling hot August day. Hoping to catch the hint of a lake breeze, I had left open our front door. Only a screened partition stood between me, inside, and any possible intruders.

About to ring our bell, the salesmen suddenly scurried away with nary a backward glance. Puzzled but relieved, I wondered why their sudden departure. Then I noticed. Chuckled.

Resembling a mini-dragon, our teenage son's pet iguana--- Drako--- clung to the top of the screen. Sharp claws gripped the fine wire netting. Beady eyes scanned tall trees with luscious leaves growing on our front lawn. Over 2 feet/0.61 metres long, including his long tail, Drako appeared an ominous creature to any unsuspecting onlooker. Like me, Drako obviously had hoped to catch a welcome breeze on the screen. Instead, he caught the eye of a couple of unsuspecting humans who fled as if seeing a monster.

How did Drako become part of our busy family that included three teenage males? Unfortunately, our middle son learned early in life he was allergic to furry creatures. No stately cats. No bounding dogs. No fluffy bunnies. So he chose an iguana. An iguana that was given freedom to roam our four-bedroom, two-storey home. But that's another story.

Not especially cuddly, Drako did, however, possess other positive attributes. Herbivorous, he loved munching on crisp, water-laden lettuce fresh from the refrigerator. Or juicy grapes accidentally left on the kitchen counter. He didn't cost a fortune to feed.

Arboreal by nature, he often climbed the floor length curtains to straddle the top of drapery rods. Nothing more disconcerting than having the feeling something--- or someone--- is watching you. Then you look around and there! on top of the curtain rod! lies a bright green lizard nonchalantly peering at you with big bug-out eyes.

With a tendency to skitter across the floor with remarkable speed---and with the flexible body of a reptile---Drako could easily disappear if not watched and be lost forever: out an open door, down a loose floor grate, or perhaps wedged behind the furniture. This became a problem because he had no scent and therefore could not be tracked down.

One afternoon, Son Owner checked his special aquarium with the lava hot rock and found **no iguana**! Raising the alarm, he enlisted his family's aid in joining a house-wide hunt for his mini-dragon. Even brought in a large, reckless tracking dog to sniff him out but with no scent to follow this proved fruitless. Only thing this rambunctious dawg accomplished was terrifying the rest of us and probably drove Drako deeper into hiding.

Desperate, we called the pet store owner who gave precise directions on how to find the reptilian pet. After filling a tin foil pie plate with water, we placed it on the floor surrounded by newspaper. Sprinkled flour on the newspaper. Now all we had to do was wait for Mr. Iguana to come out of his hiding place to drink water. Naturally he would splash in the water. Naturally his wet clawed feet would pick up the flour as he headed back to his hiding place. All we needed to do was follow his flour-laden tracks and presto! we would find him.

Except the plan didn't work. It had been one week since the mini dragon disappeared.

Until one morning we heard a shriek. Aha…Mr. Iguana must have reappeared! In Son Owner's bottom drawer of his dresser. Hidden comfortably amongst his underwear.

Drako caused cocktail chatter. Guests arriving in our home for refreshments were puzzled by many bare green stalks planted in pots. Our resident mini-dragon had polished off the foliage leaving only the stems.

It was easy to get rid of an undesirable guest. We merely introduced our lizard in all his reptilian glory. Amazing how said guest suddenly remembered something left cooking on his stove at home and hastily excused himself.

Even the twittering birds perched on the hydro wire stopped their chirp chattering in silent awe when they spied this strange creature. In a group, they scuttled quickly in the opposite direction along the wire while staring at this harnessed green iguana slowly climbing to the top of our backyard cherry tree.

When Son left for university, he found a home for Drako with a local avid naturalist who introduced myriads of students to such stunning marvels of nature as iguanas.

And Drako lived happily ever after.

A WISE OWL?

For many years Burrowing Owls captured my imagination. I first heard about this crazy little creature a long time ago on a CBC program describing the plight of Burrowing Owls in Saskatchewan. I remember thinking at the time, someday I'm going to investigate this little-known phenomenon.

After all, owls nested in trees and behaved like other owls.

Not quite. On our cross Canada drive, after entering Saskatchewan, we sought out these little feathered friends at a poorly located interpretive centre. We had to double back because we missed the small sign announcing its location amidst a barrage of other large markers.

These little creatures are cute. The burrowing owl:

-nests underground instead of trees

-is smaller in size than pigeons

-has long stick-like legs

-hunts as much in the day as at night in summer

-mimics the rattling hiss of a rattlesnake's tail (to scare predators)

-is one of the most endangered birds in western Canada

Why does this little fellow/female nest underground? A dangerous habit I would think.

Wherever it lives in western Canada, the burrowing owl uses the abandoned burrows of ground-dwelling mammals (badgers, prairie dogs) to rest, nest, and store food.

It relies on short vegetation and tall, weedy areas within 2 km of the burrows in its search for food like insects and rodents. It also needs an open terrain to watch for enemies (like larger owls!).

So what happens in winter? We know Canadian western winters can be mighty frigid and foreboding...especially to little creatures living underground!

Well, around September, the little owl begins to migrate to the milder west coast, or head across the border (like people snowbirds) to south Texas and central Mexico---a distance of 2500 – 3500 km!

Many burrowing owls that breed in Canada do not return. Only half of the adults come back to their northern breeding grounds.

There is so much more to learn about these fascinating little feather friends. They're interesting because they are different.

To me, the burning question is why are they endangered? At one time the Burrowing Owl was common in the four western Canadian provinces. Their numbers are now vastly reduced because of you and me. With our chemical pesticides we have poisoned some, killed by eating strychnine-covered grains. These very same pesticides also kill small rodents on which the Burrowing Owl feeds.

Human interaction often proves fatal, too, through vehicle and farm equipment collisions. Believe it, the little creatures are even recorded as victims of aircraft collisions!

Most often, though, the owl's decline is the result of changes in the prairie landscape. Over 75% of our native grassland has been cultivated; 40% of our wetlands lost. We all know our planet needs help. Let's not forget these little creatures.

After all, if we don't care, then whoooo will?

UNITED STATES
Robert the Haunted Doll

He's known as the world's most terrifying doll. People familiar with him insist Robert the Doll is haunted: responsible for all kinds of mysterious mishaps including car crashes.

Nonsense!

Not.

For we have suffered under the spell of Robert the Doll's curse each time we visit---or try to visit---Key West, Florida.

Our misfortunes began several years ago after viewing the weird-looking, three-foot- high, life-size doll on display at the East Martello Museum in Key West. Having heard about Robert's reputation and seeing the actual doll, fashioned from cloth and stuffed with straw, dressed in a sailor suit, we both arrogantly dismissed its/his supernatural powers as "absolutely ridiculous". No intelligent person could fall for that hocus-pocus stuff.

Except… we had openly voiced our disrespect to Robert in front of it/him. A no-no, confirmed museum staffers.

That was the day, after visiting Robert, that we lost the keys to our condo, had a flat tire on our rental car, and carelessly misplaced some cash.

My husband and I looked at each other. Not possible. This rag tag doll can't possibly hold supernatural powers. Never mind that every year tens of thousands of people pay to see Robert. He receives one to three letters daily, mainly apologies from visitors whose bad turn in life is blamed on their disrespect to the creepy doll. We dismissed all this evidence: until our cursed trip to Key West the next year. Our early morning Toronto-Atlanta flight would arrive in time to board a direct flight to Key West for mid-afternoon arrival. And glorious sun!

Not.

Because the airplane could not land due to inclement weather, our flight was diverted to Columbia, South Carolina. Five hours waiting in the plane on the ground. True, the pilot kept us dutifully updated; we were plied with foil-wrapped sweet and salty airline snacks (of which we soon tired) and water. By this time, we knew our chances of getting to Key West the same day were next to nil.

Finally, given clearance, we arrived in Atlanta. A mess! Every re-directed flight had been pushed back. Airport concourses were jammed, in near chaos, with kilometer long lines of passengers, many with babes-in-arms, trying to rebook through hapless, overworked agents.

Discovered via machine we had been rebooked by the airline for the next day but each on separate flights. Hanging on to a "may we help you?" telephone receiver forever, while partially standing in an endless line, my husband managed to secure a flight together the next day at noon.

Now for accommodation. With hundreds (thousands?) of stranded passengers, could we possibly find a place to stay the night? (miraculously, we did.)

Suddenly, separately, but at the same time, we looked at each other. Is this the continuing saga of Robert's curse, we impishly suggest? Surely not! But any disrespect to that weird-looking doll results in documented bad luck. World travelers for decades, we have never run into such a conundrum of flight associated problems at one time.

Next, we began to track our luggage. Clearly tagged for Key West. How did it end up in Miami?

We left home on a Saturday. Arrived in Key West one day later. Luggage did not appear until Monday noon: two days astray.

So…whom/what do we blame? The airline? Bad weather?

We shudder to admit this but….it was probably the curse from that insidious doll… Pardon me---I should never have written that---it's time we visit and humbly pay our respects to Robert.

GREECE

How We Lost our Way on a Small Greek Island

Our first mistake was getting off the mini-bus too soon. Wrong stop. We are on Symi, a former natural sponge harvesting island in the Aegean Sea, not far from Rhodes, Greece.

Picturesque? Yes, especially if you remain within the confines of the colourful semi-circle harbour surrounded by brightly painted homes that appear precariously perched on rocky ledges and outcroppings up the hill. The eye delights at the structure, composition, and colour of Symi's many steep hills.

I am sure when the many day ferries return to Rhodes in mid-afternoon with their hordes of passengers, the Symiots breathe a sigh of relief. They may need/want/appreciate the money, but most must also value their sense of space and aloofness. As overnighters, we realized how peaceful was the island scene when the daily barrage of tourists disappeared.

Distinguishing characteristics of Symi

A small, dry island in the Aegean Sea not far from Rhodes and the Turkish coastline, Symi is eight-miles long, crowded with 180 churches, chapels, and monasteries. Once home to 22,000, the island now has a permanent population of about 3,000.

To the naked eye, Symi often appears inhospitable and impassable, with winding roads disappearing into rocks, shale and high cliff faces at every turn. The hardy visitor is challenged/invited to ascend 500 or so white-washed steps winding up from Gialos, the popular harbour, to the old, upper village of Chorio. These 500 steps -- the celebrated *Kali Strata* -- were built by rich Symi merchants in the 19th century to link the old Chorio with the new mercantile, harbour area of Gialos. In fact, these two upper and lower neighbourhoods are each different areas of one whole.

View from the top

Once at the top, we meandered among the labyrinth of narrow cobblestone walks between centuries-old stone walls, and became completely disoriented and lost. Our goal was to discover the island's archeological/historical museum, plus a white with blue-trim church (Magali Panagia) and the remains of an ancient castle (Kastro). The castle was built by the Knights Hospitaller on the remains of an ancient acropolis from 5th century BCE. Unfortunately, the Germans destroyed it during World War II.

Photo op heaven? Our thoughts exactly. But we made a big mistake. We decided to forego the 500 straight-up steps and instead, take the hair-raising mini-bus ride to the top thus giving us more time to wander the landscape without having to recover from the climb.

Except we got off at the wrong stop.

The Misadventure

It is mid-afternoon on a sunny autumn day. Along with other locals, we sit on the Symi mini-bus with an experienced (we hope) driver who will soon steer up and around god-awful corners and hair-pin bends without guard rails. As we ascend to the top via multi switch-backs, I stop looking at the death traps below each curve. Instead, I decide to leave myself in God's hands like the elderly local man sitting across from me who makes the sign of the cross on his forehead at each bend.

Because we cannot speak Greek – and because we do not ask questions but should – we follow the crowd. It appears everyone is getting off the bus at Pedi, a lower elevation seaside village. Like lemmings, so do we. Slightly bewildered, we realize too late this is not our destination. When we finally figure this out, the mini-bus has long gone.

"Why didn't you ask the bus driver?" I ask.

"Why didn't you?" retorts my husband.

We call a truce. My Beloved checks the google map on his cell. (*How did travellers make out before cell phones?*)

"We just follow this road to the top."

Ah, but the google map does not show the steep topography of the land.

Still, the temperature is a pleasant 27 C. And the sun sparkles everywhere, as if a sea nymph waved her wand. We begin walking up the steep hill on a sort-of paved road towards our destination. Which we cannot see, of course, because it is hidden between and above hills. Then we begin to sweat. Our thigh muscles start to protest. The road is narrow. High speed motor bikers, who roar past leaving us coughing in their dust, are the only traffic.

On and on, up, up, up, we trudge. And struggle. Passing rundown ancient stone homes, abandoned auto wrecks, the occasional farm horse gazing strangely at us. A long-haired goat. Chalky roads, sparse, dry, foliage. Nothing but rocks. All shapes, sizes, and muted colours of grey. We must be in a valley since shale, scree, crushed stones, loose rocks, and sheer cliffs surround us.

The sky, however, is blue. More than blue. It is magnificent: azure, lapis lazuli, aquamarine, stunning. The brilliant sun amid this brilliant sky clearly defines the high hills and jagged rock cliffs in three-dimension.

I fall behind. Tired. Hot. Sweating. Thirsty. Slugging water from the plastic bottle I am carrying. My lightweight camera now weighs a ton.

My Beloved waits for me to catch up. I wave him on. My energy is sapped.

Finally, I reach him as we both encounter a cluster of ancient looking stone homes and a conglomeration of meandering dusty streets marked with signs. In Greek, of course.

Oh gawd, some of the roads are cobblestoned, branching off into different directions. And always up. Then to the right. To the left. Then up again. Like a giant jigsaw puzzle on a slanted table.

Exhausted, we stumble across a variety store. Seemingly in the middle of nowhere. However, we deduce from a few signs that we have, indeed, reached Chorio, the upper neighbourhood above the harbour. Remember the 500 steps? These join the upper and lower towns. Too late, we realize it would have been shorter to take them. Instead of struggling up thousands more steps in the hot afternoon sun across the spine of the island!

Bus Stop Symi

Beside the store sits a sheltered bus stop with a wooden bench under a protective wooden ceiling. We squint at the torn and worn timetable tacked to the interior wall. It appears a bus does come by this very spot every hour each day.

The bus stop recalls a favourite book, "Bus Stop Symi" by William Travis, written in 1970 and the reason Symi is on our bucket list. At the time Travis and his wife were the only foreigners to live among the Symiots. In it, Travis writes about two bus shelters, a gift from the heart by an American in Iowa in honour of his Symiot grandfather. The problem? Symi, in its earliest days, had no road and no buses so the bus stops, enthusiastically and politely received, were useless white elephants.

Today, however, there are buses and roads and so finding a bus stop in Chorio gave me concrete assurance that we could find transportation back to the harbour.

Now that we know we are not stuck here forever, our spirits gain energy and momentum. Our initial goal had been to wander through a 5-room historical museum in Chorio that received glowing reviews from other travellers.

Museum: not

Lucky us! We spy some amateur style signage: black paint on an ancient rock wall that reads 'museum' in English. Then an arrow. More uphill climbing past a taverna, winding in and around additional old stone alleyways and narrow cobblestone streets. Up, up, up. I am really dog tired.

"How much more?" I whine.

Norm checks the google map. "Well, according to this, not far. But it's very convoluted."

I mutter silent obscenities.

After an unreasonable length of time and faithfully following one sign after another (is this someone's idea of a joke?), we arrive at the Museum entrance. Another foreign couple is standing there, too. The door is closed.

"She closed the museum 3 minutes ago," said the male half of this American couple. "We got here just as she was locking the door. Something about an appointment she had to keep."

"What?!" we cry in dismay and outrage. "How can that be? It's only 3:30. The museum is supposed to be open!" We both pound on the pair of heavy wooden museum entrance doors to the amusement of our thwarted compatriots. "Open up!" we demand. Like wailing kindergartners.

Eventually, for only a minute, a woman cautiously opens one half of the double green painted door. Just a crack. "Sorry," she smiles frostily. "I have to close early today."

I am a woman of infinite patience. But I am aghast at this unwarranted rejection. I open my mouth to protest and then quickly shut it. What's the use?

"Probably a government employee," mutters my Better Half.

Reluctantly – our furious energy must be saved -- we turn to leave. Along with our US counterparts. We are disgusted this museum keeper of the keys has this miserable power over us. Why, we came all the way from Canada, the others from the U.S., to see this historic museum!

Trying to find our way back to Point Zero, the bus stop, through the maze we had just covered, required the combined intelligence of we four able-bodied but exhausted tourists.

Up, up and away...again

My husband, accepting the museum rejection, has now turned his sights on getting to the crest of Chorio village to view the castle ruins and close to it, the white and blue-trimmed church,

Megali Panagia. The church, next to the castle ruins, was also unfortunately destroyed in WWII, although later rebuilt.

Finally, after separating from the two Americans due to our slow descent and reroute through the maze, we rediscover the Bus Stop. "You go ahead, I'll wait here," I eagerly suggest. "Remember the last bus down leaves in an hour! We don't want to miss it!"

The Waiting Game

My Beloved disappears between two meandering cobblestone streets while I sit down to wait. And wait. And wait.

After a reasonable length of time, I begin to worry. He is not back. Did he fall and sprain his ankle? Or worse? Highly possible in this labyrinth of broken stones and sudden dips in ancient paths. We cannot connect with our cellphones because I have forgotten the Greek telephone company code to unlock mine. I sit in this beautiful historic place and fret. Walk up and down the narrow stone street. I glance at the slowly sinking sun. Finally, I approach the lone female vendor in the variety store next to the bus stop. My pathetic question as to how to search for my husband is difficult to convey. I cannot speak Greek and she cannot speak English.

"How late are you open?" I do manage to get across this question, pointing at her wristwatch.

Somehow, she understands and haltingly says: "Til 10 p.m. But…" someone else is coming to relieve her at 6 p.m. I have visions of spending the night on the wooden bench at the bus stop. I cannot leave without finding out what, if anything, happened to my husband. My anxiety increases. As clever as he is, he sometimes has a weakness with directions.

Suddenly I glance down the narrow-walled street. Slowly winding its way around the curve is a blue shirt. The kind My Beloved is wearing. Is it…? Yes, it is him! And he is ecstatic. He found his castle and the church atop the high hill. He was the only one there. He took photographs to his heart's delight and then decided he had better get back.

However, that meandering maze of ancient narrow streets proved a challenge to him, a fact I feared. He did manage to recognize a few landmarks and then tried to follow them back to the bus stop. Only he could not remember where to turn until he met an islander who pointed him in the right direction.

Just in time. The mini-bus arrived. We thankfully sank into one of its seats for the heart-stopping winding trip back to the harbour. Giddy with fatigue.

After the driver snaked back down the hill to his bus stop on the harbour, we asked him (he spoke excellent English) how long he has driven this crazy route up and down this unforgiving landscape.

"About 7 years," he replied nonchalantly. And yawned. His shift was over.

Fairyland

That evening we dined at a harbour restaurant on grilled calamari and small fried shrimp -- an island specialty called *simiako garidaki* or tiny fried shrimp. One eats the entire shrimp, tails and all - no peeling! -- washed down with copious amounts of dry white wine.

Looking up into the surrounding steep hills with splashes of bright, twinkling lights in old stone houses, we thought we had landed in a magic Fairyland.

Postscript

Adventures, like getting lost, help keep one nimble and young-at-heart. As travellers in our eighties, we follow Betty Friedan's creed: *Ageing is not lost youth but a new stage of opportunity and growth.*

FRANCE

POSTCARDS FROM FRANCE

Blurry-eyed after a transatlantic flight, I collapse in the airport chair to reconnect my fuzzy brain. A flurry of bright colour flashes by. My bagged eyes follow. She could be a butterfly; her floor-length peacock blue African native dress, splashed with iridescent orange and brilliant yellow flowers, rustles through the drab interior of the waiting room. Golden bracelets, hoop earrings. Matching exotic headdress sits high on her regal head, black hair peeking, falling over smooth brown skin. Fleshy, big-boned, she commands attention. Except a large, frayed elastic bandage encircling her right ankle---bare feet stuffed into a pair of jewel-encrusted sandals---ruins her royal image.

Welcome to Charles de Gaulle airport in Paris. Local time: 5:00 a.m.

It's noon. We are hungry. Dash into a local *boulangerie*. With loaded baguette in hand, we grab a small table outside the shop to munch food in the sun. Then we see him watching us. Trim black beard, straight back, he sits proudly on the curb, scarf wrapped around his worn suit jacket. Empty paper cup on the sidewalk before him. Dependent on the generosity of strangers.

We share half our lunch.

Later, on *le Metro*, a young father holding a bottle of half-finished milk while cradling his sleeping infant, lurches down each moving subway car. In his hand, an empty paper cup. Waves it from passenger to passenger for coins.

In Avignon, closer to the Mediterranean Sea, main streets are dotted with similar silent, docile figures: young, old, male, female. A constant reminder of those less fortunate. We enter a *patisserie* to purchase a *croissant chocolat.* We also buy a slice of pizza. The pizza is for the young woman sitting cross-legged on the curb outside the bakery. Lowering her head, she murmurs *merci.*

The faces of migrants.

We are at Gare de Lyon in Paris, preparing to board the highspeed train to Avignon in southwest France. A lonely grand piano sits unattended in the centre of the waiting hall. Until a youth, about 12, sits on the piano bench, and amidst the hub-bub of travellers, begins to play. Beautifully. His train arrives; he quickly departs. Soon after, another traveller sits at the waiting piano. With easy familiarity, his fingers slide over the keys playing a classical piece. Then his train arrives. He departs. And so it goes…a continuous, melodious piano concerto in the middle of madness in a local train station.

Now our train is ready for boarding: *Voiture* 6. We walk along the platform. Walk endlessly, dragging our luggage along the full length of this long train. We cannot find Car 6. In stumbling high school French we ask directions from one of the few attendants. He points backwards.We hustle back. Time for departure is near. We do not see *numéro 6.* Ask again. More pointing back from where we have already dragged our luggage. Not much time. We run. Dragging off-balance luggage behind us. Desperate now. Finally choose any car, no idea what number. Ask a stranger on the *voiture.* She scans our tickets. *Oui,* she says, *c'est le numéro 6.*

Fall asleep. Exhausted. Wake up three hours later in *la gare* Avignon.

And we still have no idea how to find the number on a French highspeed railway car.

Sur le pont

Ever been disappointed when you finally reach a travel destination that's been on your bucket list forever?

Happens all the time: a monument is not as large as you imagined. *Trevi Fountain* is smaller than you thought. The grand dinner in the oldest restaurant in France is not as great as you expected.

For us, it was The Bridge in Avignon, France, over the Rhone River. Or, as I knew it in rhyme in our French class in elementary school---

> *Sur le pont d'Avignon*
>
> *On y danse, on y danse*
>
> *Sur le pont d'Avignon*
>
> *On y danse tout en rond*

To be sure, the bridge is there. But it is only half a bridge!! Who would have thought?!

Shock was my initial reaction. This was a famous song about a famous bridge. But the bridge is only half a bridge? What kind of bridge is that?

The story slowly unraveled as we listened to its history. It was, indeed, a construction marvel: 22 arches over 950 metres (3,000 feet) spanning the Rhône River. Yet it was only 2.5 metres (8 feet wide). So how could a circle of people even dance on it?

Construction of the bridge began in 1177, presumably due to a young shepherd, Bénézet, whose visions claimed he was sent by God to build a bridge in Avignon. Completed in 1185, the imposing landmark has since been named a UNESCO World Heritage Site.

But why only half a bridge?

In 1226, after a terrible siege the city suffered under Louis VIII, three quarters of the bridge was destroyed. A few years later, despite it being forbidden, the people of Avignon put themselves to the task and rebuilt it.

From the 17th century on, the city could no longer bear the costs of the bridge's maintenance and repairs. In 1603, following strong flooding of the Rhône, one arch collapsed, then three others in 1605. Due to the plague epidemic, repair work didn't start again until 1628. Finally, the bridge re-opened in 1633. Two months later, two new arches were swept away by the Rhône. That's when city leaders decided enough was enough and they left the bridge as it is today.

Is it worth a visit? Absolutely. There is much more history to this famous bridge in this famous city and you would cheat yourself if you didn't stop in Avignon. Explore this mediaeval city of marvels. You will not be disappointed.

THAILAND

THE ELUSIVE ELEPHANT

"Come 'ere! Come 'ere!"

One of our tour companions waves excitedly. Points. We rush to where he's standing. Hopeful.

"Right there! See them trees moving! Right there!"

Squint into the bush. Shade eyes from scorching sun. Nothing.

"Aw. Gone now."

"See anything?" I ask.

"Naw," he confesses. "Just moving leaves. Had to be an elephant."

Sure, I think with skepticism. This guy probably sees Casper the Friendly Ghost rising out of a pumpkin patch on Hallowe'en.

We're on a wild elephant safari into the Thai jungle at Kuiburi National Park. Chose this tour because there was a chance we might actually see elephants in their natural habitat. After researching these majestic mammals, we decide this is the way to go even though we are warned we may not see any. Luck and being in the right place at the right time is our mantra.

"Twice as many elephants work in Thailand's tourism industry as the rest of Asia combined, with the vast majority kept in severely inadequate conditions.... When not giving rides or performing, the elephants were typically chained day and night, most of the time to chains less than three meters long. They were also fed poor diets, given limited appropriate

*veterinary care and were frequently kept on concrete floors in stressful locations." ***

At our next jungle stop, our group of 8 jumps off, scans the horizon in anticipation. We are on a plateau overlooking a large treed valley. Suddenly a flock of white egrets erupts from distant tree tops.

We do know there is a symbiotic relationship between egrets and elephants. Egrets get a free ride and meal from insects the elephant kicks up as he moves across the jungle floor. In return, the egret feeds on parasites living on the elephant. We mention this quietly to our hyper tour friend.

"Elephants!" he suddenly screams to everyone. "Those white birds mean elephants!"

Not necessarily but possibly. The white birds we spy are far in the distance. Trying to spot an elephant in a treed jungle from our lofty vantage point is impossible. Our motormouth friend has stirred up a hopeless hope.

We mutter: "this is the afternoon. Animals and birds are usually active in the early morning or evening. Any elephant is probably resting in the shade out of the hot sun like any sensible creature."

And so, as the afternoon wears on, our hopes diminish for seeing an elephant in the wild. But we continue to wait. And look. Scour the landscape. Walk back and forth across the cliff top.

Close to twilight now. Park closes at 6 p.m.; insects already feasting on unprotected tourist flesh. Reluctantly we climb aboard the back of our safari truck. Slowly the driver retraces our rough and muddy route.

"Stop!" orders a half whispering, half shouting guide with skillfully trained eyes. Points into the jungle to her right. Sun beginning to set. Rays act like an illuminating backdrop.

Scanning eyes, cameras ready, silence. Ignore bug bites.

Guide points again. Straining eyes catch a large, round gray mound amidst trees in the distance. It moves!

Yes! See him! See his tusks! About 100 metres! Chomping on leaves! Ambling through his natural habitat! Unaware of spying human eyes!

Cameras click in unison.

"Madame," cautions the guide respectfully. "No flash please!"

Damn my camera!

Group stands in back of panel truck. Mesmerized. Watch every move Babar the Elephant makes as he slowly, languidly, eats his way through the foliage, ambling across our muddy trail in full view about 80 metres behind us. Then he blissfully wanders into the bush, disappears from view.

Giddy. Thrilled. Worth the heat, bugs, discomfort, mouthy tour companion.

The elusive elephant.

*World Animal Protection (WAP) report

MADE IN THAILAND: Snapshots of Life and Love

Office in the Airport

An obese woman, sitting on the cool, tile floor, one leg tucked beneath her massive bottom, the other straight out in front, her back leaning against the full-length glass window, is dozing. She catches our eye in Bangkok's Suvarnabhumi (say that in a hurry) Airport because we are waiting, bored, for our highway bus connection to our destination after a long flight. Our rental condo is four hours away in Hua Hin, on the Gulf of Thailand.

She is amazing, this woman who looks in her thirties. Wearing black slacks, a black and white polka dot top, black slip-on shoes, she remains alert despite her closed eyes. Round owl glasses sit on her pug nose. Short, curly hair surrounds her round face while her pudgy fingers (a gold band adorns her ring finger) keep tabs on three steadily ringing cellular phones.

She answers each cell as if in a fog, automatically grabs an official-looking form from her 'desk' (an overturned plastic stool on the airport floor), scribbles words with her left hand into appropriate spaces, ends the call, motions to a lurking young male assistant who goes running off with said paper to where? The activity repeats itself with each new cell call. The three cells ring continuously.

When she can't stand the rings any longer, she reaches for a full roll of toilet tissue, places it on the chair seat in front of her, leans her forehead on the roll using it like a soft pillow.

This woman is conducting some sort of travel business in this busy airport, oblivious to the hustle and bustle. Her bag of belongings lies scattered around her. No-one dares enter 'her' space.

She has created her own office with no overhead. And she appears to be thriving. She is an original Made in Thailand entrepreneur.

Thai woman, white man

We see these couples everywhere. From previous research, I know many websites   promote endless romantic possibilities for a foreign man with a nubile, beautiful, young Thai girl.

But what catches my eye are the high numbers of these mixed couples. I am curious. The Thai girls are young; the foreign white men to whom they are attached are old. And not good-looking or suave. They have overhanging pouches, some can barely walk, and some are not gentlemen.

I watch these mismatches dine together. We are at the next table. Young Thai girl and old man barely say a word (language is obviously a problem); the girl invariably grabs the man's hand throughout the meal as if he's about to escape. He pays the restaurant bill, of course. They leave hand-in-hand.

I watch in the telephone office when speaking Thai makes business sense. While my husband struggles to purchase SIM cards or figure out what numbers to use for North America with a Thai sales clerk, the old man standing at the clerk next to us turns his problems over to his Thai girl. She handles the transaction. Acts as interpreter, takes his credit card, and if he protests about costs he doesn't understand, she quickly holds his hand to calm him. Then she slides off the stool still holding her high-end shopping bags, links her arm through his, and off they go to spend more money.

We walk along the beach where these young girl/old men couples are a common sight. She is completely clothed, covered from top to bottom so no sun rays can age her virgin skin. Skin on his chest burned red, he wears his teeny tiny Speedo bathing suit, gut overlapping the waistband. Their hands are romantically linked as they putter along wordlessly.

In the mall, these couples are everywhere. Young Thai girl is petite, barely up to his stooped shoulder. In one hand he holds many packages from expensive boutiques. His tiny Thai lady grips his other hand tightly. No conversation passes between them.

As a stranger in these here parts, I am not criticizing. Rather, I am fascinated at this growing phenomenon.

Why do I have this nagging feeling that Cupid did not fire any arrows? Perhaps for young girls, the motivating force that binds is money (or the promise of), an escape from poverty, or just wanting to leave Thailand for a new life in a new land.

As for the old men, this is probably what they want and need. A Made in Thailand partner.

The Fruit Lady on the Thai Beach

"Madam, you want I cut up your mango? You want I roast your corn…open your beer?"

Kohsoom (meaning *lotus* in Thai) is a welcome addition to this gorgeous beach at the end of the lane that runs alongside our condo complex in Hua Hin on the Gulf of Thailand. She is a remarkable reminder that when life hands you lemons, you make lemonade.

Kohsoom, she of the laughing black eyes and a smile as warm as the Thai morning ocean breeze, is mother to 4 children, one of which---a girl---has gone with her ex-husband. "I no see her again," she laments, quickly changing the subject. With 3 children by her current husband, Kohsoom sells fruit and drinks to throngs of tourists who flock to this popular 4 km long beach fronting turquoise ocean water with a sandy sea bed.

One of Thailand's many poor, Kohsoom's story unfolds little by little as we chat with her day by day. She lives on the beach with her 3-year-old son, *Noon*. From early morning until almost dusk when tourists desert the beach, Kohsoom serves from her stand while Noon plays around her. Every day except Wednesdays. All year. For five years now. A small round grill to roast corn nestles close to the sand. The ubiquitous tools of her vendor trade are scattered around her postage size site: cooler, trailer she hitches to her motorbike, large open umbrella, plastic chairs, plastic water bottles, table and knives for cutting up the fruit, garbage can, and those inevitable, environmentally-damaging plastic bags.

She works hard, this lady, charging less for a standard Styrofoam tray of freshly---and neatly---sliced mango, jackfruit, watermelon, pineapple…slightly undercutting the shiny new market stores in nearby malls.

The Big Boss collects an annual "minimal" sum for her small patch of sandy beach, she says. Her husband, one of a group of Beach Patrol Volunteers who ride horseback (each owns his/her horse) along the beach, is obliged to pay half his profits from horseback riding to the Big Boss. Each morning, before he heads off on his horse, he rakes the sand on her territory and helps set up her stand. Each night, they take it down.

Despite precautions, she must also guard against thievery "by my own people". Although the couple dutifully chains their meagre belongings securely to a nearby tree overnight, covering their belongings with a tarp, they are robbed. "We knows who does this," she shrugs. "They bad people." All part of living on the beach.

It is young Soon who captures the tourists' attention. They buy him cold treats from the visiting ice cream truck. Bring him toys. When his sisters are home from school and at the beach with their mom, they play house on the concrete lane and sandy beach. Large banana leaves transform into plates. Bougainvillea blossoms, shells, rocks magically resemble a food feast. Mini sea crabs sometimes capture Soon's imagination as the tiny crustaceans skitter, scatter to and from their hole homes, forming raised grid patterns across the beach. And, oh yes, the mobile phone gives Soon lots of electronic exposure. The kids ignore the sea, the turquoise sea tourists pay mega bucks to experience.

Weather elements play a big role in the Fruit Lady's business. And with the health of her family. When the temperature is in the mid-30s from morn til dusk---when afternoon winds kick up into ferocious velocities allowing kiteboarders to leap and dash and fly across the ocean surface---and your life is on the beach, it's not so good for little Soon. "He get fever from wind. Heat not good," she says. We feel the boy's forehead. Hot. Hot. Hot. He lies listlessly in the trailer. Half-sleeping. Whimpering in a never-never land.

She powders his face. And hers. To protect their skin from the relentless sun.

The beach is a hive of activity: horseback riders, kiteboarders, sun worshippers, sun strollers, clothing vendors. A background for professional wedding photos. And if you hanker for some relaxation, *Meow Massage* beckons with shaded tables.

In the end, though, the Fruit Lady epitomizes the beach. She grabs many foreign hearts with her honest, genuine style. "I make okay living," she says. "Save for my children." Pauses. Flashes a smile showing even white teeth.

"Yes. My children. So they grow up good. To study."

Manor House / 905-648-4797
www.manor-house-publishing.com